For little letters everywhere —D.U.

For all those who work to break down walls —J.H.R.

Dial Books for Young Readers

An imprint of Penguin Random House LLC, New York

Text copyright © 2020 by Deborah Underwood

Illustrations copyright © 2020 by Jiae Hwang

Visit us online at penguinrandomhouse.com

Library of Congress Cataloging-in-Publication Data is available.

Printed in China

ISBN 9780525554028

5 7 9 10 8 6 4

Design by Jennifer Kelly

Text set in Chronicle Text G1 Roman

The illustrations in this book were created digitally, with the help of ProCreate and all the letters from A to Z, both big and small.

every little letter

by Deborah Underwood

illustrated by Joy Hwang Ruiz

Dial Books for Young Readers

Once upon a time,
there was a city of letters
surrounded by walls.

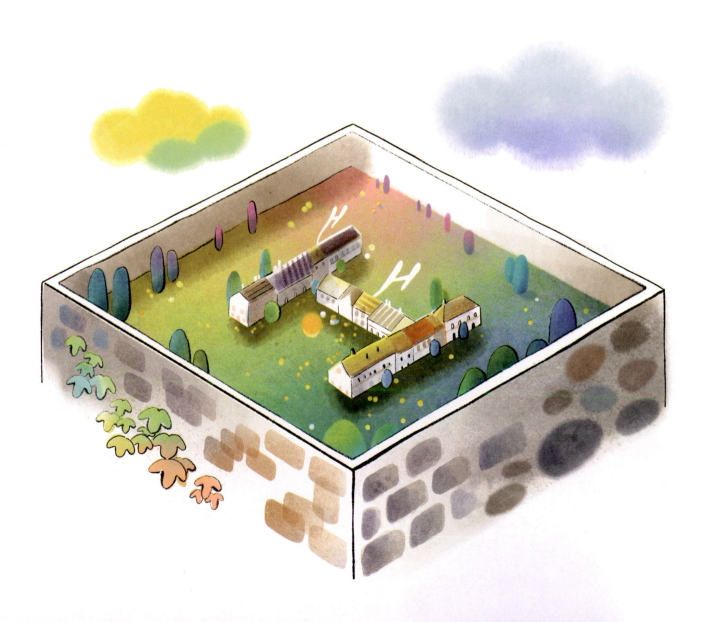

The letters were all the same.

Their conversations were pleasant . . .

but not very interesting.

The H's felt safe behind their walls.
They knew other letters lurked outside.
Different letters.

The H's had built the walls around their city
long ago to protect themselves.

And the H's were happy enough.

Except for one small, curious h.

She wondered what the other letters looked like.

She wondered what they ate.

She wondered if they even existed.

One day, the small h found an opening in the wall.

She peered through it . . .

and saw an i.

The i did not look
dangerous.
It did not look scary.

The h slowly reached
her hands through the
opening.

The i reached out too.

And together,

they made something

extraordinary.

But a big H saw

and soon the wall
was sealed up again.

The small h
missed her
new friend.

She had an idea:

She sent him
some letters.

LOTS of letters.

But one flew astray.

The idea spread from one small letter to another.

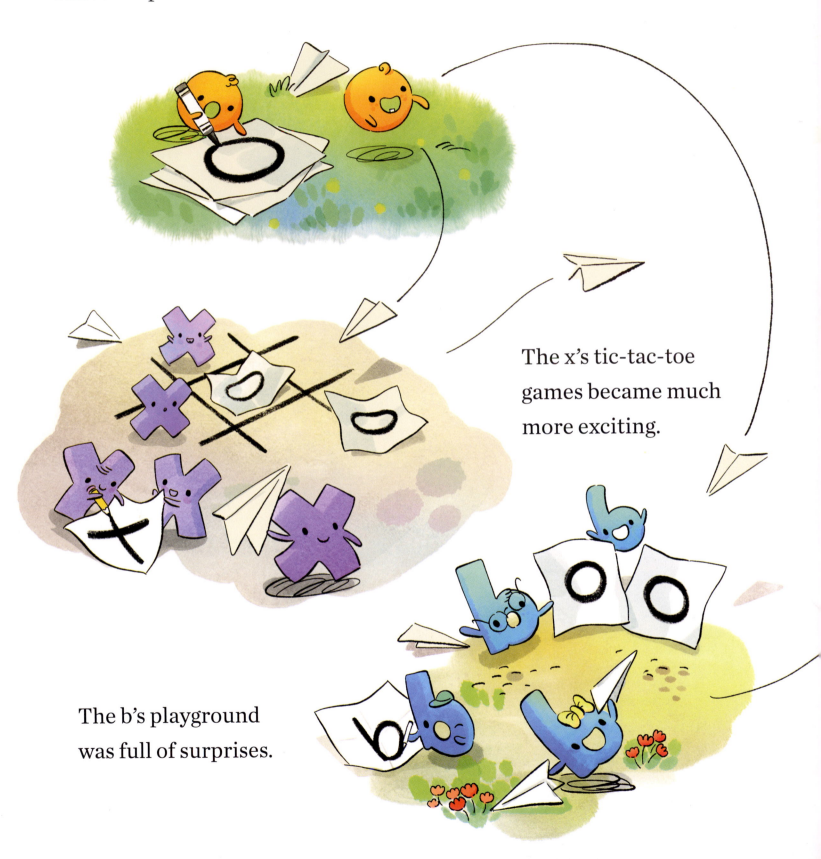

The x's tic-tac-toe games became much more exciting.

The b's playground was full of surprises.

And the y's finally got some answers.

But the big letters found out.

The little letters had no words to describe their sadness.

The h had only a small d and a small n she'd managed to hide away.

Why were the big letters so afraid? The situation seemed hopeless.

Until ...

she looked at things differently.

The h spread the word.

Night fell . . .

and day dawned.

But the big letters were still afraid.

Until one reached out.

Then another.

And another.

How do you tear down walls?

With words at first.

Then brick by brick.

After the walls came down, the letters were silly together . . .

and serious together.

And finally, together, they discovered . . .

the most important word of all.

The OXFORD Treasury of
WORLD STORIES

Oxford University Press, Great Clarendon Street, Oxford OX2 6DP

Oxford   New York
Athens Auckland Bangkok Bogota Buenos Aires Calcutta
Cape Town Chennai Dar es Salaam Delhi Florence Hong Kong Istanbul
Karachi Kuala Lumpur Madrid Melbourne Mexico City Mumbai
Nairobi Paris Sao Paulo Singapore Taipei Tokyo Toronto Warsaw

and associated companies in
Berlin Ibadan

Oxford is a trade mark of Oxford University Press

British Library Cataloguing in Publication Data
Data available
Library of Congress Catalog Card Number: 98 – 5385

Cover illustration by Liz Pyle

ISBN 0 19 278144 8

Typeset in Bembo
by Mary Tudge Typesetting Services

Printed in Europe

The OXFORD Treasury of
WORLD STORIES

Michael Harrison & Christopher Stuart-Clark

Oxford University Press
Oxford New York Toronto

Contents

Anansi and the Banana Bird

A STORY FROM THE CARIBBEAN

ANANSI THE SPIDER was always eating. He enjoyed eating all the fruits of the jungle—and he especially liked bananas.

The Banana Bird also liked eating bananas. He even had yellow and black feathers so that he looked like a banana.

Well, the monsoons had nearly finished and the bananas were just ripening when Anansi met the Banana Bird.

'Hey!' called Anansi. 'If you weren't moving I'd have thought you were a banana. Be careful when you're standing still—someone might eat you! I enjoy eating bananas myself.'

'Ha, ha! Always the funny one, aren't you?' replied the Banana Bird, rather offended. 'I may look like a banana—but I bet I can be first to the bananas on Mr Brown's plantation.'

'I wouldn't be too sure about that,' said Anansi. 'I can get about faster than you think.'

'Well, let's have a bet. Let's meet up at Mr Brown's plantation, where there are lots of bright, fresh bananas. The first to get there can take away and eat as many bananas as he likes.'

'Done,' said Anansi, rubbing all his legs together with delight. 'But I warn you, when you get there I will have already arrived with time to spare.'

'We'll see,' said the Banana Bird. 'At least we'll find out if you know how to eat bananas without being caught.'

'Just you wait,' said Anansi, and gave the Banana Bird a curious look.

Banana Bird was sure he could arrive first by flying to the plantation. So he was in no hurry. He looked about among the trees, he rested in the branches of the mango tree, he pecked at the cocoa plums, he

perched on a branch and let the sea breeze blow through his feathers. And only after jumping around on the beach for a while did he begin to fly to Mr Brown's plantation.

The banana plantation was huge—you could not see all of it at once. The Banana Bird asked a goose and a goat on the way about the brightest bananas. He followed their instructions, and came to perch in a tree overlooking the plantation. When he got there and looked down . . . there was Anansi, in among the bananas, quietly eating.

The Banana Bird was so surprised that his wings became tangled in the leaves of the trees and he landed with a bump on the ground in front of Anansi.

'What's this?' asked Banana Bird angrily.

'This? Well, these are bananas, and they are just ripe,' answered Anansi.

'I know perfectly well they're bananas,' said the Banana Bird, raising his voice angrily. 'You know very well what I want to know—how did you arrive here before me?'

'That's easy,' said Anansi. 'While you were wasting time in the trees, preening yourself and looking for other fruits, I spun and spun and wove threads together to build a large web. I climbed and climbed, not thinking about anything else until I had reached the top. Then I found the bananas.'

'But I can fly! You don't have any wings!' cried the Banana Bird indignantly.

'And for every leg I have more than you, I can spin more web and get wherever I'm going faster,' replied Anansi, biting into another banana.

Laughing to himself and moving his legs to a rhythm, Anansi began to talk and gradually turned his words into a song:

Banana Bird, you could have been first,
But you came out worst!
You should always use your head,
And not just your feet.
You perch up there and you go tweet tweet,
I used my head and I used my feet,
And that's how I beat
The Banana Bird! Banana Bird!

Banana Bird did not want to listen any more. Angrily, he took off into the air and lost himself in the banana fields.

Anansi laughed loud and long. Then, because he could not take all the bunches of bananas, he tore off four bananas that looked the ripest and set off for home.

When he arrived home he asked his wife to cook the bananas, drank some cocoa to refresh himself, and fell asleep under the shade of a palm tree.

As soon as the bananas were ready he gave the largest to his wife, the other three to his three children, and stayed empty-handed himself.

'Do you want some, Daddy?' asked the children.

'Do you want some, Anansi?' asked his wife.

'I want some,' he said, pretending he did not mind, 'but there were only four bananas and it is better that I go hungry.'

'No, no,' they all cried. 'Have half of our bananas.'

So they each broke their banana in half and each gave half to Anansi.

And Anansi sat up—and started eating again. So how many more bananas did Anansi get than his wife and three children did?

The Two Cats

A STORY FROM IRELAND

BROTHER FELIX should not have been in the convent. He was the only male who lived there with all the nuns. Father Patrick came each day to say mass, and sometimes he stayed for a cup of tea, but Brother Felix lived his whole life inside the walls and wandered where he would. These days he wandered very little, having grown old and stout.

He had first come to the convent as a little kitten, years ago it was, and was called Sister Felicity, until it was obvious he wasn't. He should have been turned out at once and for good, driven away, but the nuns had grown fond of him and he was allowed to stay. He had been a good cat, always bringing the mice he caught into the chapel and laying them on the altar steps as his offering to God.

But, but . . . Years passed and he grew lazy, and he grew bad-tempered, and he grew demanding. 'My milk! Now!' he would shout. 'My supper! Now!' And he went on shouting, even in chapel, until one of the sisters gave him what he wanted. It was usually Sister Faith who had to attend to him. She was the youngest nun in the convent and got the worst jobs. Looking after Brother Felix was definitely the very worst job of all now that he was fat and demanding and smelly, and inclined to scratch if he didn't get exactly what he wanted. Sister Faith grumbled gently to Father Patrick that she hadn't become a nun to look after a bad-tempered old cat and I suspect that some of her prayers suggested to God it was time for Brother Felix to join him in heaven.

It was worse in summer. Brother Felix had always loved to climb the yew tree in the middle of the convent garden and sun himself and keep watch over his empire. Now that he was grown old and fat and lazy he found it troublesome to climb down the tree and, instead, shrieked imperiously to be fetched.

It's not easy climbing a tree when you wear a nun's clothes and Sister Faith was a resourceful woman. She tied a piece of old clothes line to his favourite branch.

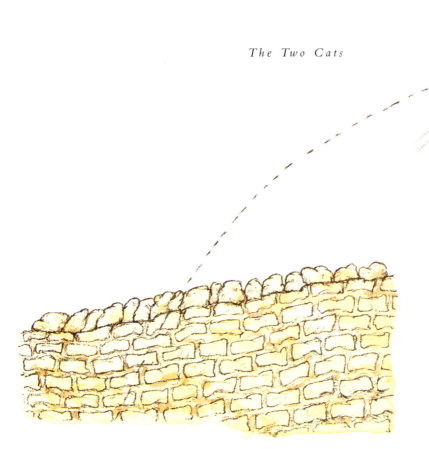

When he shrieked now she pulled the rope until the tip of the branch touched the ground and Brother Felix could waddle slowly down.

One hot day Sister Faith had already been called out of chapel twice by Brother Felix when she heard his awful shrieking from the yew tree. She walked into the garden in the full heat of the late afternoon sun and took hold of the rope and started to pull it down. The branch was nearly on the ground. Brother Felix had stood up ready to waddle. It must be that Sister Faith's hands were sweaty in the heat and slipped on the rope. It must be; she was a nun, and good.

Sister Faith's hands lost their grip. The yew branch sprang upwards. Brother Felix was catapulted through the air, over the chapel roof, over the convent wall, and was never seen again. Sister Faith was, of course, very sorry indeed, very sorry. She was still sorry even when she had to look after the fluffy little Sister Leonie that Father Patrick brought to the convent. She told Father Patrick that looking after a little kitten wasn't likely to make her a good nun, it was too pleasant and easy. How good for her, she said, Brother Felix had been.

[13]

Father Patrick smiled. He was wise and used to keeping secrets, and he went between the convent and the town. That very morning he had met old Mrs MacKeever puffing up the hill with her shopping bags. Out of one of them peered a rather familiar-looking face, as bad-tempered as Mrs MacKeever's was beaming.

'Father, a miracle,' she said as soon as she could get her breath back.

'I see you have a new cat to replace your old Tom,' Father Patrick said.

'A new old cat,' beamed Mrs MacKeever. 'You know how, when you told me I must get a new cat to replace old Tom, I said I could never manage a little kitten now, all frisky, out all the time?'

'Yes,' said Father Patrick, 'but it's all right. I've found a new home for the little kitten after all. The nuns have taken it.'

'Well,' said Mrs MacKeever, 'as I was passing the convent last week I paused, and opened my arms and I said out loud, "I do wish the Good Lord would send me my old Tom back!" when, at that very moment, a cat fell from the clear blue heaven, right into my arms. A nice, comfortable old cat to keep me company. We're on our way to the fishmonger now to choose his supper. Isn't that a miracle indeed?'

'Indeed it is,' said Father Patrick. 'Indeed it is.'

Robin Hood and Sir Richard Lee

A STORY FROM ENGLAND

ROBIN LEANT AGAINST THE TRUNK of the oak tree. Its rough bark eased the itch in his back, but not the itch in his mind.

'You are poor company,' he said to his men. 'You tell the same stories, laugh at the same old jokes—it's time we had company for dinner. I swear I will not eat until you have found a guest for my table with an interesting story to tell.'

His men walked through the trees to the edge of the forest. The dusty brown road curved away, empty. The peasants would all be in the fields.

[15]

Only the idle rich would be on the road, and there weren't many of them. They could have a long and hungry wait before their dinner with a reluctant guest.

But they had not been there many minutes before a little mist of dust showed someone was coming, someone on a horse, someone with money. As the rider came nearer they saw it was a very sad-faced knight who was riding along in dreary clothes and on a bony horse. One push from Much the Miller's son and he would have been sprawling in the dust of the road—and his clothes wouldn't have looked any different, for they were dusty, dull, and worn.

Will Scarlet stretched out his hand and held the horse's rein. The rider looked up slowly and stared at them. Then he laughed, a sad laugh. 'Look out!' he said. 'I'll be robbing you. You've stopped the wrong man if you're looking for money.'

'We're not looking for money,' Little John said, 'but for someone to dine with us and amuse our leader, Robin Hood.' The knight seemed

unable to protest any more as he was led into the forest, but walked with them until they came to the outlaws' camp: rough shelters made from branches covered with wilted bracken, a fire smouldering in a ring of stones, a leg of meat dripping fat noisily into it, a tall, thin man sitting against a tree in the shadows.

Robin scrambled to his feet and came towards them. 'Welcome to my hall,' he said. 'I am Robin Hood, Lord of the Forest. Who honours my table today?'

'My name is Sir Richard Lee,' the man replied, 'and I am very glad to be offered food at your table.'

After dinner Sir Richard thanked Robin for the excellent meal he had given him and for the good company that had lightened his spirits.

'Now you must pay,' said Robin. 'No knight leaves my table without paying for his meal, and paying well; and if you cannot pay in silver, then you must pay in words and tell us your story.'

'I must pay with a story, then,' Sir Richard said, 'and my story will tell you why I cannot pay with silver. My troubles are not my fault. They began a year ago. It was my son, my heir—but now there is nothing left to inherit. He is a young man of twenty, and had been a good boy, never in serious trouble. Then, on his birthday, there was some jousting in the nearest town and he went, just to enjoy his day. That was the last day we have enjoyed . . .

'My son won his first joust. Then he was drawn against a knight from Lancashire. By now the ground was muddy, the horses tired. As they rode towards each other my son's horse slipped. He found himself falling and twisting in the saddle. He wrenched himself upright but in doing so his lance grazed the back of the other knight. He in turn fell, and fell under the hooves of my son's horse . . . and was killed.

'The umpires declared that my son had deliberately struck his opponent on the back. To buy his pardon I had to raise a large sum of money, all that I had, and more. I borrowed from the abbot of St Mary's Abbey in York and gave him the deeds of my land as security. I had a year to pay him back but illness and bad luck have dogged me. I am travelling now to beg the abbot for more time. If he does not grant it, then I have lost everything.'

'And is the abbot a good Christian man?' asked Robin.

'He is a very rich man. And I think he loves his riches.'

Robin laughed. 'I think he had the pleasure of giving gold to me not long ago,' he said. 'Perhaps we might give him back his gold—if he is a good Christian man. Suppose I were to lend you the money you need, what security could you give me?'

'Nothing but my word, by Our Lady, whom I love.'

Robin smiled. 'That is enough for me,' he said, 'but we must test this abbot of yours.' He sent Little John to dig up four hundred gold coins and put them into Sir Richard's saddle-bag.

'I will go as his squire,' said Little John, 'just in case he should meet some wicked outlaws as he travels through the forest.'

Sir Richard stood amazed, tears running down his cheeks. 'I will be back on this day twelve months from now,' he said, 'to repay you every penny.'

'Let me tell you what to say to my lord abbot,' said Robin. 'If he is a good Christian man then I should not have robbed him. You can test him for me.'

So Sir Richard walked into the hall of the abbey on the day appointed, dusty from the road. Little John stood just outside, careful. Too many people in York might want a word with him. At the high table sat the abbot and his justice, a crooked weasel of a man. They looked up as Sir Richard approached and saw rich lands coming into their grasping hands.

'Well,' said the abbot. 'Sir Richard Lee, I think. Dear me, is a year passed already since we last had business together?'

Sir Richard fell on his knees. 'Father, in the name of Christ's blessed Mother, I beg you grant me more time. I have had bad luck and sickness this year but I will be able to pay in just a few months. For pity's sake, a few more months.'

The abbot smiled. 'My son, it is God's will. Sickness and misfortune are signs of God's displeasure. How can I go against the will of God? If he had wanted you to pay off the loan in time, then he would have sent you the money. As you cannot pay me, your lands are forfeit and will serve this abbey and the greater glory of God.'

'How can I fight against the will of God?' said Sir Richard. 'As you say, if he had wanted me to pay you, he would have sent me money.'

Saying this, Sir Richard pulled his leather bag from under his cloak, untied the strings, and cascaded the coins over the table and into the lap of the abbot.

'There, your money in full. God's will be done!' and he took up the deeds to his land that were on the table and walked away leaving the abbot and his justice open-mouthed behind him.

Sir Richard and Little John laughed all the way out of York, and then they parted company. Little John was going back to the forest. Sir Richard was going home. He had to raise the money to pay back Robin Hood within the year, as he had given his word. They would meet again next year after many adventures, but that's another story . . .

The Fox and the Tomten

A STORY FROM SWEDEN

IN WINTER, when the hard frost turns the trees white and the ground is covered in frozen snow, it is beautiful if you only have to look at it. But if you have to go out to find food it makes matters very difficult . . . especially if you are a fox.

At other times, Fox can move around the forest and he is not easy to see; but in winter he is far too obvious in his red coat against the bright white of the frost and snow. So when he goes hunting he has to be even more careful than usual.

[23]

When evening comes, Fox has to leave his den to find something
to eat for himself and his family. He has to come out of the forest—
although he will be easy to see. He knows he must find food and he
has to creep silently towards the farm where he will find chickens.
But humans may easily see him if they look out of their warm homes.
It may be dark on a winter's evening but the frost and snow seem to light
everything up.

Tonight it is very light. The snow is white and the sky is bright—you
would not think it was night-time at all. Fox wonders to himself, 'Will
anyone see me? There is a light in the window of the house—I hope no
one will look out to see a hungry fox coming through the snow.'

But someone can see him.

It is the old Tomten, who watches the farm at night.

In the farmhouse the children are playing and soon it will be their
bedtime. They do not know about the fox. But they believe in the
Tomten and they are sure that he guards the farm at night. They have
never seen him, but they know he comes. And every night, before they
go to bed, the children put out some warm porridge for the old Tomten
by the back door of the cottage.

Fox is nearer to the farm now. He walks slowly round to the
cowshed—there must be something here for a hungry fox to eat. It is
night-time, it is quite quiet, the cows are asleep—what do they care
about a fox?

The mice in the cowshed are wide awake. 'Come on, Fox, try and
catch us if you can! You can try but we have a hole in the floor so we
can escape you. Ask the farm cat—she knows. Come on, Fox, catch us if
you can.'

But Fox does not want to catch mice. He is not interested—there
are many other things that taste much better. He is creeping towards
the hens.

There is a fluttering and a squawking in the shed where the hens
live. They have heard Fox coming. They give out loud cries of fright as
he comes nearer.

But then there are footsteps outside. The hens hear them . . . and the
fox hears them. The hens are quiet. The fox is quiet. Who is this coming
through the snow?

It is the old, old Tomten, who guards the farm at night.

'Hello, Fox,' he says. 'Were you frightened? Have you not seen
me before, going round from this building to that building on the farm?'

[25]

But the old Tomten knows that the fox is hungry. 'What are you doing near the hens? You know that no one is allowed to steal our hens, don't you?'

'I wasn't going to steal your hens,' says the fox. 'I would not dream of stealing hens.'

'I saw you poke your nose through that hole in the shed where the hens are,' said the old Tomten. 'But while I am around all those hens can sit safely on their perches and sleep at night.'

Fox looks sad. But the old Tomten knows that Fox is hungry.

'Here, look,' he says. 'The children in the house always leave me porridge outside. They have never seen me but they know I am here. You eat this.'

The fox begins to eat the porridge—it is very good.

'It's good, isn't it?' says the old Tomten. 'You can share my porridge. You can share it every night, if you like. But you must not touch our hens.'

'We'll see about that,' says the fox. 'But thank you anyway.'

No longer hungry, and feeling happy, the fox goes back to the forest and through the forest to his den. He goes carefully, as the morning star can already be seen above the edge of the forest.

In the morning the children come down and see that the porridge has been eaten.

'The Tomten's been!' they shout. 'Look! The Tomten's been and eaten the porridge.' But they never know about the fox.

[26]

The Frog Princess

A STORY FROM RUSSIA

'IT IS TIME that each of you found a wife,' said the tsar to his three sons.

'How do we set about choosing the right girl?' asked the eldest son.

'Each of you must make a bow, take an arrow, and shoot it away into the distance. The girl who brings you back your arrow will be your wife.'

The sons were surprised at their father's suggestion, but they felt that they should obey him—or at least try his method out; so each found a stout branch from a tree and made a good, springy bow, chose a straight, smooth stick for an arrow, and prepared to shoot—for a wife.

The eldest son shot an arrow away into the distance; his arrow was brought back by a princess.

The second son shot an arrow away out of sight; his arrow was brought back by the daughter of a general.

The youngest son, Prince Ivan, then shot an arrow away into the air; he waited and then his arrow was brought back . . . by a frog.

The two eldest brothers were very happy with the way things had turned out and were soon married. But Ivan was certainly not very happy and went away wondering how he could marry a frog.

He was very sad and also jealous of his two brothers with their fine-looking wives. But in the end he quietly married the frog.

The tsar now decided to find out which of his new daughters-in-law was the most skilful; so he asked them each to make him a shirt so that he could compare them.

This was not so easy for Ivan. 'What can my frog make which will please my father?' he said to himself, watching his frog creeping around the floor and croaking. 'Everyone will laugh at her—and at me.'

But when Prince Ivan fell asleep the frog shed her frog skin and became a beautiful girl. Her name was Yelena. At once she clapped her hands and called out, 'Servants! Bring me a shirt fit for the tsar!'

Some small frogs that were hiding by a nearby pool then turned into Yelena's servants. They brought her a shirt of the highest quality, and she took it, rolled it up, and put it near the sleeping Ivan. Then she and her servants turned back into frogs.

When Ivan woke up he was amazed to find the beautiful shirt beside him. He took it to the tsar, who exclaimed, 'This is a magnificent shirt. I shall wear it on all the smartest occasions.'

The second son brought a shirt that had been made by his wife, the general's daughter. It was a very plain, ordinary shirt. The tsar told him, 'I could never wear this shirt in public.'

When the eldest son brought his shirt which had been made by his wife, the princess, the tsar found it was made of many pieces of different cloth and not even sewn properly. 'I shall never wear this shirt,' he exclaimed.

Soon the two eldest brothers got talking together.

'It looks as if we were wrong to be laughing at Ivan's wife,' said one.

'She must be a witch, not a frog,' said the other.

Now the tsar announced, 'I want to see which of my daughters-in-law is the best cook. Each of them must bake me some bread.'

The wives of the two eldest sons were determined not to be fooled again. 'Let's send a woman to spy on this frog and see what it gets up to,' they said.

But the frog noticed that there was a spy. So she did a very strange thing. She took some dough, broke off the upper part of her stove, and poured the dough into a hole in the ground.

The woman who had been spying went back to the two wives and described exactly what she had seen. The two wives were rather surprised but they did exactly what had been described to them.

The frog smiled to herself. Then she turned once again into the beautiful Yelena and called her servants. 'Bake me some bread,' she said, 'like that which we give my father on Sundays.'

The frog-servants quickly brought the bread. Yelena took it and placed it near Ivan's bed; then she turned into a frog again. When Ivan woke up he took the bread to the tsar. He found his father was already trying the bread made by the other two wives. Because they had followed what they were told the frog had done, their bread was—not surprisingly—uneatable.

'I cannot eat this!' cried the tsar. 'Let us hope that Ivan's wife can do better.'

After he had tried the bread made by the frogs, he said, 'This is delicious! This is the bread we must serve at all ceremonies and all festivals!'

Finally one day Yelena decided to show herself to Ivan as a princess before turning back into a frog. When Ivan met her he did not know who she was.

'Ivan. I am Yelena, your princess. You think I am a frog, but I can change into Yelena and back again.' And then she turned back into a frog.

Ivan was so happy with his frog-princess wife. But he wanted her to stay as the beautiful Yelena and not turn back into a frog. So the next time she turned into a princess, Ivan saw the frog skin lying on the ground, took it up and—when she was not looking—burned it.

When Yelena began to look for the frog skin she could not find it. 'I have burned your frog skin,' Ivan told her. 'Now you will stay as my beautiful Yelena for ever.'

'Oh, Ivan, you should not have done that!' she cried. 'You should have been patient. Now I have to leave you. Goodbye! You will only find me now at the other end of the world.' And with a cry of despair she disappeared.

Ivan was heartbroken because he missed Yelena so much. But as time passed he not only recovered from his great sadness but became determined to see if he could find his frog-princess. So he decided to go off in search of her.

He had travelled a very long way when he came to the back of a small cottage at the edge of a wood.

'Cottage!' he said. 'Turn around and face me.'

The cottage suddenly grew feet and turned round and Ivan entered. Inside he found an old woman.

'I smell a Russian,' the old woman said. 'Hello, Ivan. Where are you going?'

'Please give me some food and drink first, old woman, and then I will answer your questions.'

So the old woman gave him some bread and some water and made up a bed for him. Ivan then explained that he was searching for his wife, the frog-princess, the beautiful Yelena.

'I don't know her,' said the old woman. 'Perhaps my elder sister does. You must go and see her. Follow this path and you will find her in another cottage, just like this one.'

After a good night's rest, Ivan set off for the old woman's elder sister. As the old woman had told him, he came to another cottage.

'Cottage!' he said. 'Turn round and face me.'

This cottage also grew feet and turned round and Ivan entered. Inside he found an even older woman.

'I smell a Russian,' the old woman said. 'Hello, Ivan, where are you going?'

'I am looking for my beautiful Yelena.'

'You are just in time. She has nearly forgotten you; and she is going to marry someone else. The wedding is very soon. You must go and see her—she is living with my other sister, the eldest of the three of us. Now listen carefully. As soon as you enter the house Yelena will turn into a spindle. My sister will spin a golden thread. As soon as she has

finished she will put the spindle into a trunk and lock it. You must find the key, unlock the trunk, take the spindle, and break it in two. Throw one part in front of you and one part behind you. Then Yelena will appear again.'

Ivan set off for the cottage belonging to the eldest of the three sisters.

'Cottage!' he said. 'Turn round and face me.'

Again this cottage grew feet and turned round and Ivan entered. It was just as the second old woman had said. There was a very old woman spinning. She worked very slowly and could hardly see. He watched carefully—when she finished she put the thread and the spindle carefully into a trunk and locked it. Ivan saw where she put the key, and when the old woman hobbled slowly out of the room he unlocked the trunk, took out the spindle, broke it in two and threw one piece in front of him and the other behind him.

At once Yelena, his frog-princess, appeared.

'Ivan! Why did you wait so long? I am soon going to have to marry someone else,' she cried and rushed to him. 'Quick! Stand with me on the old woman's carpet.'

They both stood on the carpet and held each other tightly. The carpet began to move and they flew away, back to the home of the tsar.

Yelena's days as a frog were over. And as for Ivan—he never looked at another frog.

The Three Wives

A STORY FROM ITALY

THERE WAS ONCE A KING who had three sons. They had squabbled as babies, they had fought as children, and they were icily polite to each other as young men. The king, who was as wise as kings in stories always are, feared for the peace of his kingdom after his death.

He decided that his sons should marry and that he would then set the couples a test and the winners would be king and queen after him. Two of the sons agreed cheerfully, each convinced that he would win.

The middle son had read all the stories and knew that he would win nothing, but he couldn't expect to be king anyway so he agreed resentfully.

Choosing brides was not as simple as it sounds. Each brother watched the others and as soon as one began to make advances to a young woman, the others would pursue her too. Their rivalry grew fiercer and the king feared that, whoever won, there would be accusations of unfairness.

He summoned his three sons on to the palace roof and gave them each a sling and a differently coloured stone: blue for the eldest, green for the middle son, and white for the youngest.

'Where the stone lands, there you must find your wife,' the king said. He did not think that any young woman would refuse to marry a prince, however disagreeable he was.

The three slung their stones, watched where they went, and set off with their best smiles ready. If they could not find a willing woman they could not enter the contest. The eldest saw his stone on the roof of the weaver's house. He had a daughter of the right age and so that was all right. The youngest son was the next to find his stone, in the doorway of the baker's shop, at the feet of the baker's daughter, so that was all right.

The middle son slouched through the town. His stone was nowhere to be seen. He went through the town gate and there, just outside, there it was, in the ditch. There were no young women there—it was much too muddy a ditch—but there was a frog. The middle son sat down and laughed.

'Hello, Frog,' he said. 'Are you a beautiful princess in disguise? Shall I kiss you?'

He bent down, half believing the old stories, and gently kissed the frog's damp lips. Nothing happened. The frog sat and looked at him and he sat back on his heels and looked at the frog.

'Oh well,' he said. 'It was worth a try. Now what shall I do?'

Really, he was now out of the contest but he did not want to see his brothers triumph over him, so he walked back to the palace looking as cheerful as he could and just smiled when his brothers asked questions and boasted of their own successes. 'A country girl,' he said to his father when he asked.

The king now announced the contest, and you might think it was unfair, if you didn't know how just kings always are. He gave each son a fleece of wool and told them to bring it back spun and woven by their young woman. The finest cloth would be the winner. The eldest son hastened to the weaver's shop, confident indeed. The youngest son went to the baker's, thinking all women can spin and weave and so he had as much chance as his brother.

The middle son took his fleece back to the ditch outside the town wall. He was surprised to see the frog still sitting there. 'Here we are,' he said. 'I'm afraid you've been asked to spin this and weave it as fine as you can.' He tucked the fleece into the fork of a walnut tree growing on the bank and wandered off into the countryside.

When he came back the frog croaked at him. He looked into the tree and found the fleece was gone. There was a walnut in its place, wedged in. He put the walnut in his pocket, said, 'Goodbye, Frog, and thank you!' and wandered back to the palace.

The other two brothers came back several days later with parcels of cloth. The weaver's daughter had, of course, woven her wool as fine and soft as silk and the eldest son knew that he must have won the crown. The baker's daughter had tried, had really tried, but her cloth was a mass of knots and lumps, and loose ends.

'And you?' the king asked, turning to the middle son.

'This is mine,' he said, and put the walnut on the table. Everyone smiled. It was a gracious way of conceding defeat. The king took his nut-crackers and broke the nut open. Cloth spilled from the nut, slithering silkily over the table, across the floor, seeming to fill the room.

'There's no end to it,' the king said and at that very moment the end of the cloth dropped out of the nut shell.

'The second test,' said the king, thinking fast, as kings do and realizing that he really loved his youngest son best, 'the second of the three, is to take one of these puppies each and to bring them back in a month. The best dog will win.'

The three brothers set off as before. There were no pets in the weaver's house as they would just spoil the precious cloths they produced but the weaver's daughter found the puppy a box and put it in the yard, and did her best. It survived, but only just, and was rough and wild and surly when it came back to the palace. The baker's shop had lots of dogs, to keep the rats under control, and it was bright and fit after its month.

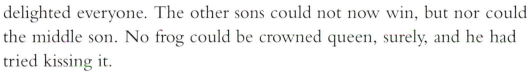

The middle son produced another walnut.

There was expectation when the king cracked it open. Out trotted a tiny dog that begged, and trotted, and delighted everyone. The other sons could not now win, but nor could the middle son. No frog could be crowned queen, surely, and he had tried kissing it.

'Finally,' said the king, now wondering whether the middle son might not have something to be said for him after all, 'the final test. You will all be married tomorrow. The finest wedding dress and carriage will equal the two earlier tasks, and the most beautiful woman will be what decides it, if the scores are then equal.'

The middle brother wandered back to the ditch. The faithful frog sat there. 'No walnuts, this time,' he said. 'We're to be married.'

He took a lily leaf, for that seemed somehow to be what the frog wanted and put it down on the road. He found four snails and tied them to the leaf. The frog hopped on to the leaf and they all set off for the palace, slowly, very slowly indeed.

They had moved a few metres towards the gate by nightfall. Try as he could he could not walk as slowly as the snails so he would walk ahead a few paces, and then sit and wait for them to catch up. Several times he fell asleep. When it grew dark he walked as far as the gate and lay down in its shadow and slept deeply.

He was woken by a tickling in his ears and warm breath on his face. A horse was nuzzling him gently. He looked up and saw four horses, a golden carriage, a beautiful young woman in a lily-green dress. She stretched her hand out of the window.

'Come and join your frog,' she said. 'I was put under a spell by a jealous witch . . .'

'. . . until someone would marry you as you were,' finished the middle son, who had read all the stories.

As you have read the stories you will know that they became king and queen and the whole kingdom lived happily ever after, unless, of course, they did any of the things you mustn't do in stories.

Flood

A STORY FROM SOUTH AMERICA

THE TWO BROTHERS were in the fields with their llamas. Suddenly, one of the llamas spoke. That in itself was surprising enough, a peaceful beast you have taken to graze on the mountainside for years suddenly talking. More surprising was what it said:

'We must go up to the mountain top, now.'

Most surprising of all was the reason it gave. 'The world is going to be flooded.'

The two brothers looked at each other, and laughed. They were high up the great mountains already. It was many days journey down to

the lowlands, weeks to the sea. Where would water come from to
flood all this land? The seas were busy enough keeping themselves
full of water, kept sucking it from one place and putting it down in
another, then rushing back to move it again. They certainly didn't have
any spare.

'Come,' the second llama said, and both animals turned and trotted
up the mountain. That decided it. If they lost their beasts they were done
for and they ran after them. Worries about llamas which start talking
nonsense could wait.

The two brothers followed them up the mountain, up and up as it
grew steeper and steeper. The llamas stayed just out of reach, bounding
ahead one moment, stopping to nibble the next. They left the village far
below, the trees, and even the plants, and still the llamas went up,
scrambling over the mossy rocks, the bare rocks, until there was no more
up, and very little room.

The talking llamas were just the first of that day's surprises. Perhaps
even more surprising was that they never, ever, spoke again.

As the two brothers stood getting their breath back, or trying to in
that thin air on the high mountain peak, they thought at first the ground
itself was moving up towards them, a flood of earth it seemed. As it drew
closer they saw, not earth but animals, all the animals in the world, two
of each, flying, running, hopping, creeping, crawling, until they arrived
at the very top.

The last and biggest surprise of all was by now no surprise at all.
The sea followed the creatures up the mountain: the wild, green sea, salt
spume blowing, waves breaking, walls of water roaring up the mountain.
Nothing but heaving wet stretching as far as you could see. The sky
seemed full of water too: black clouds, driving rain.

They all huddled together on the little peak of rock on top of the
world of water. The two brothers tried not to think about what had
happened under that advancing flood and of what was going to happen
as it came higher, and higher.

It didn't come higher. It stopped and lapped at their feet, like a
too-friendly dog. They all stood and stared at it, hoping it would go
away. It stayed, for days. They grew hungry. The foxes started to
eye the doves and edged towards them even though there really wasn't
room to move. They paddled in the shallowest edge of the sea and
their tails drooped into it and their paws and tail tips came up
black as sin and they edged their way back in fear and forgot the doves,
for now.

At last the water crept away, quietly, a bit ashamed, and left shining
black mud behind it. All the animals crept down the mountain following
the water-line and the brothers followed them, slipping and sliding.
The world was bleak and desolate.

The sun came out. Seeds stirred. Life seemed possible again, but there was nothing for the brothers to eat. The pairs of animals had spread out far away from the hut they had built and no crops were ready for harvest. They wandered further and further but just came home with a few shoots. Gradually they grew too weak to wander far and were giving up hope and began to wish they too had drowned.

One evening they staggered home, exhausted, despondent, and found a wonderful meal laid out on a clean cloth in front of their hut. They ate and ate, and when they had eaten all they wanted the food was all gone. They stayed at home the next day, hoping another meal would miraculously appear, but nothing did and they went hungry to bed again. They found that if they went searching for food they would find a meal prepared on their return but if they stayed, nothing.

One day the elder brother sent the younger out and remained himself hidden in the hut. As evening came two bright parrots flew up with a cloth between their beaks. They were spreading it out when he could restrain himself no longer but rushed out of the hut. With great squarks they flew off, pulling the empty cloth behind them.

They did not return for several days, no matter what the brothers did. Then, just as they were beginning to despair again, they returned one evening to find the meal laid out as before.

The younger brother was eaten up with curiosity and carefully arranged to hunt separately from his brother next day. He crept quietly back to the hut early and lay still and patiently. Again, two brightly coloured parrots flew down and spread their cloth. Remembering his brother's mistake, he lay still and quiet until both birds had their backs to him. Then he leapt out and seized one and held it tight.

In his arms feathers changed to skin, small parrot grew larger, and he found himself clasping a beautiful young woman and facing another, as alike as sisters. They were laughing at him. 'It took you long enough,' they said.

When the elder brother came home he found a wife waiting for him, welcoming, bright and noisy, as a wife should be. Their children filled the valley with their shouts.

Water

A STORY FROM CANADA

WATER.

Sila loved water, thirsted after it, could not live without it. All the summer days she swam in the waves' arms, her hair streaming like seaweed. In the winter gales she stood on the rocks and laughed as the waves yearned towards the shore, the fine spray running off the ends of her hair. Only the sea was vast enough and changeable enough for her. Every moment it was different and every moment it was the same. Sila never seemed to tire of it, could never have enough to satisfy her craving.

When she was a child no one worried that all her time was spent on the shore, but no one stays a child. She had no mother and no father and her five older brothers needed her to do the work that women did then: to cook, and clean, to fetch tame water in clay pots. It was hard work, it was a day's work every day, and it left no time to swim and stare and laugh with the sea. Sila drooped and dragged, and then dropped what she was doing and ran barefoot to the shore and forgot everything until a brother came and dragged her back.

They were not unkind; they needed her to work. They made her promise them she would not go to the shore and, because she loved them, she promised. Then she dreamed and in her dreams the sea called her. Waves reached out their white arms and opened their green hearts and she woke crying like the gulls. She kept her promise, but her

liveliness was gone and her life seemed to be ebbing away. They were
not unkind, her brothers.

The people's god in those first days on earth was Raven.
They turned to him and he helped them, brought fish and fire.
The brothers in their despair went to Raven and told him of their
problem. 'You cannot change what is,' he said. 'Keep your sister from
the sea and she will die.'

So Sila swam in the summer sea, in the waves' arms. In the winter
gales she stood on the rocks with the fine spray running off the ends of
her hair. She remembered her brothers, when she could, and cooked and
cleaned and fetched the tame water, when she could. It was not enough
and the brothers grumbled among themselves and added her work to
their own, for they were not unkind.

One day a wave rose up into a man, tall, glistening, with sparkling eyes and water running off his skin. He held his arms out and the sea reflected greenly off his chest. Sila stepped back and her footstep filled with water that shone in the sunlight between them. The man laughed and his laugh was like the winter sea.

'You do not remember me, Sila, yet you have been in my arms.'

Sila stared, mouth open so the salt wind savoured her tongue. 'In my dreams you have called to me,' she said.

'In the sea,' the man said, 'when you were just a child.'

Sila shook her head.

'Where are your parents?' the man asked.

'I do not know,' she whispered. 'No one speaks of them.'

'Your parents took you to see your grandmother who lived along the coast. They went in too small a boat on too rough a sea. They went under the waves. I took you in my arms and carried you to shore and set you on the sand.' Sila looked down. Her footprint had dissolved away.

She looked up. The man stood, his hand out. She took it and they played together in the sea that day and all the summer through and she became his sea-wife and loved him as she loved the sea itself and he held her as the sea held her. The cold winter seas drove him away, with many promises to return in spring. Sila stood now in winter gales and cried his name out to the winds.

When her child was born it was not as other babies are but looked shaped for the sea, seal-like and furred. Sila loved it dearly but her brothers and the other villagers shied away, fearful. Now she was often followed to the shore as if she needed to be guarded from harm, or kept at home, and she dreamed wild dreams again and cried out and her son cried with her.

When spring came her brothers were busier and could watch her less often and she and her son and his sea-father could play in the rolling waves, hair streaming like seaweed and laughing. Could play, until that day when one of her brothers, passing along the cliff-top path saw them, ran for his bow, and shot the sea-man. Blood flowed, mingling with the sea, and the sea-man slipped away as more arrows stung the water.

Sila cried out day after day, month after month, as the sea sucked her ankles, but her husband never returned. Her brothers looked uneasily at her son as he grew, for he grew as strange as he had been born. Sila feared for his life too, and one morning she led him by the hand down to the shore. 'Go,' she said. 'Swim out and find your father's kind.'

He went, and Sila sat on the sand and wept, her salt tears mingling with the sea.

There Raven found her. With one black wing he fetched the clouds down and with the other black wing he raised up the sea so that drops hung in the air, a watery world in which Sila could move and breathe and be unseen.

'This is Fog,' Raven said. 'I have made it so that you can see your son in safety. Call him, and he will come.'

Sila called into the silvered stillness, and her son came and they comforted each other until the sun melted the fog away and the men could see to work. Whenever fog came after that, Sila slipped to the shore and called and her son warmed her heart. One day she did not return, but fogs always do: water hanging in the air, like magic.

The Star-Wife

A STORY FROM SOUTH AMERICA

T HE YOUNG MAN WAS UGLY, not fancied by the girls in his village. They judged by the outside when they were young and did not value his loving heart enough. He worked his potato fields carefully, bringing baskets of earth up from the valley every year to replenish the fields he had made on the steep mountain side. Stone walls held the fields, and he felt his heart beginning to turn to stone too. The nights were the worst, and then he would leave

his empty hut and wander lonely to the mountain top and stand and stare long at the stars. They seemed so bright, so close that he could almost stretch out and touch them. Some nights silver tears would sparkle coldly on his cheeks.

One night, everything changed. He could not bring himself to look at the stars, their bright beauty that filled the sky seemed to mock his empty heart. He sat on the top of the world, his face buried in his hands, and felt himself in hell.

A touch on his shoulder made him start. He looked up. A dazzling silver light shone on the mountain top. It came from the young woman standing straight in front of him, a young woman so beautiful he could only stare.

The Star-Woman held out her hand and said, 'Will you take me home? I wish to be your wife.'

You must know that the star people can see into people's hearts, and our ugly young man had a most beautiful heart and the Star-Woman had fallen in love with him. The Star World is a land of fires of ice, and the warmth of his heart drew her to him across the sky.

He stretched out his hand and took hers. It was cold but it gripped his firmly. Her long silver hair swung as she turned her head and her clothes were like mist in moonlight. He led the way down the steep and narrow paths and into his hut. It was filled now with silvery light and he feared what his neighbours would think and say next day.

And so the Star-Wife wrapped her hair up in a scarf and put on his mother's old clothes and hid hers under the bed. Her face and hands still glowed starry silver and the young man made her stay indoors and said nothing to the villagers about his new wife but went cheerfully to his potato fields each day, and ran home each evening. His crops prospered; his house gleamed. His wife was cold, so cold, but he had enough warmth for them both. He had not known there was such happiness in this world.

But the Star-Woman was not so happy. She began to long for the dazzling whiteness of her world. The hut was dark, and rough, and grubby. No matter how hard she scrubbed, dirt would come in. The air in this mountain hut was heavy to her and sat on her shoulders, bowing her down. And, although she loved the heat of her husband's heart, the warmth of his body fevered her and his mother's old clothes scratched her fair skin.

She longed to wear her light robes and to walk in the thin air in the cool of the night. She pined and lost her sparkle.

The young man, who loved her with all his generous heart, could not bear to see her so but he knew what trouble his narrow neighbours might cause if they saw someone so strange, so different from themselves, for few people have the heart to welcome real strangers.

And so, one night, she shook loose her hair, put on her starry robes again and they walked up the steep and stony paths to the mountain top.

[56]

She flung back her head and drank in the myriads of stars above.

'Will you come?' she asked.

'Of course,' he said.

She held his hand tightly and streamed like a shooting star through the air pulling her Earth-Husband after her until they landed in her land, the land of fires of ice. The young man was shaking with the cold, shuddering as if he would come apart. She clutched him to her but her coldness made him shake the more violently and the dazzling brightness blinded him.

Nothing she could do could stop his frozen shivering or let him open his eyes. Icicles of terror sank into her heart and she knew she must take him back to his mountain.

As soon as he could speak he said, 'We must part. You can never be happy in my world, and I could not live an hour in yours.'

'I will stay, because I love you,' the Star-Woman said.

'You must go, because I love you,' he said, and she looked into his generous heart and knew that he was right. She must go, for he could never be happy if she stayed.

And now, at night, he leaves his empty hut and wanders lonely to the mountain top and stands and stares long at the stars. They seem so bright, so close that he can almost stretch out and touch them. Some nights silver tears sparkle coldly on his cheeks.

Cinderella

A STORY FROM NORTH AMERICA

T HE PEOPLE ROUND ABOUT knew him as Strong
Wind, the Invisible. He lived with his sister at the edge of
the wide bay—and he could make himself invisible when
he wanted.

He and his sister lived in a tent near the sea and his sister used to
help in all his work. Many girls would gladly have married this powerful
warrior; and when they were told that Strong Wind would marry the
first girl who saw him when he came home at night, they became keener
than ever to try to win him as a husband.

[59]

But, of course, it would be easy for any girl to say she had seen him, even if she had not; so Strong Wind thought of a trick to test whether the girls were telling the truth. Whenever a girl went down to the beach in the evening to try to see him coming home, Strong Wind's sister walked with her. His sister could always see him, but the girl could not.

When Strong Wind came home in the evening light, his sister would see him approaching and say, 'Here comes Strong Wind now; do you see him?'

And every time the hopeful girl would say, 'Yes, I can see him clearly.'

'What is he drawing his sled with?' the sister would ask.

And each girl would answer, 'With a great cord.'

So the sister would know that the girls were telling lies and their answers were just guesses. Many girls tried to win him as a husband this way, but Strong Wind refused them all—he would not have a wife who lied.

In the nearby village lived a great chief who had three daughters. Their mother had died some time earlier. The youngest of these daughters was very beautiful and kind and everyone liked her; the two eldest daughters were jealous of her beauty and of her kindness to others and they treated her very badly.

They made her dress in rags so that she looked ugly. They cut off her beautiful long black hair. They even took coals from the fire and burned her face so that she was scarred. Then, as if that were not enough, they told their father that she had done these things to herself. But the young girl stayed patient and kind and worked in the house, as she was happy to look after her father, who no longer had a wife to look after him.

[61]

Like most of the other girls in the neighbourhood the chief's two eldest daughters tried to win Strong Wind as a husband. In the evening, as the sun went down, they would go to the shore with Strong Wind's sister and wait for him to come home.

Soon he came home, drawing his sled. As usual the sister asked, 'Here comes Strong Wind. Do you see him?'

Each of the elder daughters lied and said, 'Yes, here he comes.'

'What is his shoulder strap made of?' asked the sister.

'Of leather,' said one, guessing.

'Of wool,' said the other, also guessing.

Then the two daughters entered Strong Wind's tent, hoping to see him having his supper. When Strong Wind took off his coat and his shoes, the two girls could see the coat and shoes but nothing else. So in the end they went home very angry.

One day the chief's youngest daughter, although she was dressed in rags and her face was burnt, decided to try to see Strong Wind herself. She patched her clothes with pieces of bark from trees, put on a bracelet and a necklace, and went out to try to see the Invisible One, just as so many of the girls in the village had done before her.

Her two sisters laughed at her and shouted, 'You foolish, ugly little girl! You will never see Strong Wind.' And as she made her way to the shore all the people in the village laughed at her, because of her tattered clothes and her burnt face—but she carried on in silence.

On the sea-shore Strong Wind's sister greeted her kindly; and soon Strong Wind came home drawing his sled.

'Here he comes. Do you see him?' asked the sister.

'No, I don't,' replied the girl. And the sister was surprised, because for once someone had spoken the truth.

Again she asked, 'Do you see him now?'

Then the girl answered, 'Yes, I do, and he is wonderful to look at.'

'With what does he draw his sled?' asked the sister.

'With the Rainbow,' answered the girl.

'What is his bowstring made of?' asked Strong Wind's sister.

The girl replied, 'His bowstring is the Milky Way.'

Then Strong Wind's sister knew that, because the girl had told the truth at first, he had made himself visible to her. The sister took the girl home and bathed her, and the scars went from her face and body, and her hair grew long and black again. She gave her beautiful clothes to wear and then asked her to take the wife's seat in the tent.

Soon Strong Wind came in and sat beside her and told her that she would be his bride. From then on it was Strong Wind's new wife who helped in all he did.

When their young sister did not return home the two eldest sisters were furious and wondered what had happened. Strong Wind knew how they had treated their sister, and decided to punish them. He turned them both into aspen trees and fixed them in the earth.

Since that day the leaves of aspen trees have always trembled— because they are shivering in fear at the approach of the Strong Wind. No matter how softly the Wind approaches, they always tremble, remembering their lies and how cruel they were to their sister long ago.

The Lake Lovers

A STORY FROM NEW ZEALAND

WHAT DO YOU NEED FOR A BEAUTIFUL STORY? What fits between 'Once upon a time' and 'happily ever after'? A handsome young man, certainly. A beautiful young woman, of course. And families causing trouble—that helps.

The handsome young man was Tutanekai, the youngest in his family. He was handsome, as handsome as the nights of full moon, but he had older brothers, lots of older brothers, who would always get first choice of anything. They were fishermen and lived on an island in the middle of the blue waters of the lake.

[65]

The beautiful young woman was Hinemoa. She was beautiful, as beautiful as the dawn, but she had a father who thought no young man was ever good enough for his precious girl. The family lived in the village on the lake shore and the men farmed and hunted.

One evening there was a feast in the village and Hinemoa saw Tutanekai, saw him as if for the first time, and Tutanekai saw Hinemoa and knew he must marry her. They were shy, the feast was noisy and bustling and crowded, and their families were all around them. They did not manage to speak one word to each other, but their eyes told them all they needed to know.

Every night Tutanekai sat on the shore of the island where the waters lapped at the sand and played his flute. The clear sad notes flew across the water to where Hinemoa wandered lonely under the trees that fringed the lake. She heard the music, as if the night itself was

sighing of its broken heart, and thought of Tutanekai and wondered what
he was doing and if he thought of her.

So time passed and there was another feast and this time they
managed to speak. They had time for a few words only, but those were
enough. They told their love, and they told their fears: that their families
would never let them marry each other. They longed to be together but
did not know what to do. Any sign that they cared for each other would
make Hinemoa's father lock her up, and Tutanekai's older brothers would
demand her for one of them.

'I would come to you across the water, if I dared,' she said.

'Take a canoe from the beach and come,' he said. 'We can be
together on the island. There are many quiet glades where no one
comes. I will build a hut, and fish, and we can be happy together.'

'Suppose I missed you in the darkness? How would I know where
to come?'

'Follow the sound of my flute; it will guide you to where I am.
I play to you every night already.'

'It is your flute? I thought it was too beautiful to be human playing.
It sounded like the night itself, sighing for the day.'

And then they were separated and could not speak again. Next night, as the sound of Tutanekai's flute crossed the ripples of the lake, Hinemoa went down to the shore. The canoes were pulled up on the beach, casting grey shadows under the moon. She seized one and tugged, and tugged, but it refused to move by as much as one grain of sand towards the water. She tried another, and another. Each one was too heavy for her to move.

The flute called to her, breathing across the water. The moon beams made a path across towards the island and in one mad moment she ran down to that path that led towards her love. She took two steps, and tripped, and sprawled. Her face and fingers were pressed into the fishing nets spread out to dry and she lay, like a landed mermaid, caught in man's meshes.

The nets had gourds as floats. Hinemoa untied them all from the nets and then tied them all to each other and launched herself on the water. The sound of the flute called her and the gourds held her up as she paddled with her hands towards her love.

And paddled, and paddled. The island seemed to get no closer. Her village was still dangerously near. The music cried at her and she cried in frustration back. Her arms were tiring. The cold of the water was creeping into her body and despair was sinking into her heart. It was too far for her to paddle with her hands. She could not hold her fingers together, and slowed, and slowed. Love had launched her and still called her but night and distance were winning.

She cried again, 'Tutanekai! Tutanekai!' and the breeze took her cries and played with them before dropping them at last where Tutanekai sat mournfully. He cursed himself then for his folly, for expecting Hinemoa to come to him unaided. He pushed his canoe into the water and paddled towards her village.

So it was that they met half-way, in the moonlight. He scooped her up into his canoe and paddled back to the island. His mother was waiting on the shore. His flute had fallen silent, yet he had not returned home.

She was worried about him, he had been moony lately, and she had come out to talk to him. The canoe ground into the sand at her feet and her son stood up supporting the cold, wet, exhausted young woman and she knew now what had been wrong with him and swore that they would marry.

And they did. Hinemoa's father was so impressed by her courage and determination that he, too, agreed to their marriage, for he loved his daughter and wanted her to be happy, as she was, ever after.

Ned Kelly—Iron Man

A STORY FROM AUSTRALIA

THIS WAS GOING TO BE THE 'BIG ONE'. Ned Kelly and this outlaws had been hunted like wild dogs by the police for too long. This time they would be the hunters—or so they thought. In the event it was Kelly's last stand.

It was Saturday evening in Glenrowan, a small town just north of Broken River. After the last train came through Ned and his men planned to tear up some of the track just outside the station. No trains came through on a Sunday, except the special police train. They would ambush this when it was forced to stop, round up the police—who, after all, usually rounded other people up—and then they could raid the banks freely.

[71]

There was talk in the town that a whole load of cast-iron had gone missing. Nobody could explain the theft—except Ned Kelly. He had his gang busy making strong metal armour for themselves. They made breast-plates, back-plates, and helmets: a suit weighed about forty-five kilos in all! They left their legs unprotected as they would need to be mobile and legs do not need armour when you are up close raiding a bank.

Ned called to his men, 'Round up all the townsfolk and bring them to the hotel. I am going to check the rails being ripped up.'

Some of the people of Glenrowan were happy to go along with Ned's gang. Many had heard of his daring and his humour, of how he often entertained his prisoners, of how he was quite a ladies' man. Often the poor of the community received money from his raids themselves.

When he came to the hotel Ned saw the local schoolteacher among his prisoners.

'Good to see you, teacher. I am sure you can keep all these people in order,' he joked.

'I'll certainly try to, sir,' came the reply.
But the schoolteacher was watching Ned
and his men carefully. And when Ned
suggested that they should start up some
dancing to pass the time, the schoolteacher
took his chance and slipped out of a back window—
and telegraphed a warning message to the police.

The dancing started and just as Ned was beginning to enjoy
himself, knowing that the police would soon be coming up the track,
a message was handed to him. 'So you thought you would ambush us.
We are on our way—not by train—and we know where you are.
See you soon!'

Ned was stunned. He released the local people at once, and his own
men were keen to make a run for it.

'Come on, Ned. Those lawmen have never caught us yet.'

'. . . and they aren't going to now. Let's go!'

[73]

'Wait!' shouted Ned. 'Now is the time to stand and fight and prove they can't beat us. We have our armour, we'll take them on. We won't be hunted like dingos any more.'

Suddenly a blazing torch flew through the hotel window, and a fire started. Ned's men found it difficult to move in their heavy armour and were gradually overcome by the flames. Only Ned could move.

Ned heard a call from outside the hotel. 'Come on out, Ned Kelly. We've got you at last.' The police were waiting, with rifles raised. But they were astonished by the sight that met their eyes. Ned stood in the doorway, a huge man in armour of solid iron.

Through his helmet he shouted, 'Fire away, you can't hurt me. I'm made of iron.' And as he walked slowly forward bullets bounced off him.

But one of the policemen, realizing the armour did not protect his legs, aimed at the knees, and the wounds and the weight of the armour brought Ned Kelly down. They stripped him of his armour and took him to hospital to tend his wounds.

A doctor got talking to him. 'So they got you at last. How come you didn't try to escape this time? You always managed to before.'

Ned looked at him wearily. 'A man gets tired of being hunted like a dog in his native land. I wanted to see the thing end.'

Ned was soon moved to prison. The guards there knew all about Ned's exploits. They too were curious about his capture.

'Your gang were all dead in the hotel—why didn't you leave them there and escape yourself?'

Ned looked them in the eye and said slowly, 'A man would be a nice sort of dingo to walk out on his mates.'

The Missing Gold Coin

A STORY FROM TURKEY

NASRUDIN'S WIFE KEPT NAGGING HIM. 'What is the point of being a holy man and a great scholar? You make no money by it. We are poor, poor, poor.' And she went on and on and on.

At last, one morning, Nasrudin was so exasperated that he prayed out loud. 'Lord, give me a thousand gold pieces. Surely I have earned them in your service? Just one thousand. If you give me nine hundred and ninety-nine I will not accept them. One thousand gold pieces, that is what I ask for.'

Nasrudin's wife was listening to his prayers and was happier now. She knew her husband was such a holy man that God would not refuse to give him what he asked for, in time. She was not so foolish that she expected gold coins to rain down from heaven that instant. She was kinder to Nasrudin that morning, and so from that day on he always ended his prayers in the same way: 'Lord, send me one thousand gold coins. I will not accept even nine hundred and ninety-nine.'

Nasrudin's neighbour was not a holy man, in fact he did not believe in God at all. Perhaps that is why he was a very rich man. As he listened to Nasrudin's prayer every morning he became more and more irritated. 'One thousand gold coins!' he said to himself. 'He'd be very glad to be given one gold coin! Wouldn't accept nine hundred and ninety-nine indeed!'

One day the neighbour could stand it no longer. He carefully counted out exactly nine hundred and ninety-nine gold coins into a bag and tied it up. 'We'll see about that,' he said to himself.

Next morning, when Nasrudin was in the middle of his last prayer, when he was saying 'I will not accept', a heavy bag flew in through the window, hit him on the side of the head, and clinked to the floor. Nasrudin rubbed his sore head, and then untied the bag. When he saw what was inside he lifted up his hands and said, 'Lord, thank you for answering my prayer.'

At this his neighbour poked his head through the window, laughing. 'Aren't you going to count it, Nasrudin? After all, if it isn't exactly one thousand, then you can't keep it and will have to find someone to give it to.'

[76]

Nasrudin looked at him sharply and then tipped the coins out and started putting them into piles of ten, and the piles of ten coins into rows of ten. The neighbour leant through the window, watching as the golden columns formed a square, ten by ten—almost. The last column was one coin short.

'Well, that's it,' the neighbour said. 'You said you would not accept nine hundred and ninety-nine gold coins, and that is exactly what you have been sent. You will have to return them.'

'I never said they all had to come at once,' Nasrudin replied. 'This is a test of my faith. I believe the last coin will arrive soon. I shall sit here and wait patiently until it does. How could I be so foolish as to doubt the Lord?'

The neighbour laughed. 'You are a fool to believe all that,' he said. 'Those coins did not come from God. I threw them through the window for a joke and I will have them back now.'

'I know that you threw them through the window,' Nasrudin said, 'but God used you as the best way to get the coins to me. You were acting as his agent. Anyway, it is very simple. You threw the coins in at my window. The coins are now mine. God will find a way of giving me another gold coin before long. Wait, and your patience will be rewarded.'

Nasrudin's neighbour controlled his temper, just. 'Come with me to court then and we will let the judge decide between us. I will accept his verdict, if you will.'

'That sounds very fair to me,' said Nasrudin, 'except for one small problem. You are a rich man, and dressed in fine clothes. I am a poor man, dressed almost in rags. Judges are always on the side of the rich and they will believe you rather than me. We would not stand an equal chance.'

The neighbour took off his coat and passed it through the window. 'Here, put this on. It will cover your other clothes and you will look as well dressed as me.'

Nasrudin put the coat on and called his wife in. When she saw
the columns of gold glinting in the morning sun she was speechless for
once. 'Watch this gold until I return,' Nasrudin said. 'But, mind, if
another gold coin comes through the window while I am away, send a
messenger to the court quickly, for that will be proof that it all came
from God.'

Nasrudin walked out of his front door, and at once tripped and fell.
He sat there holding his ankle and moaning. 'I'm sorry,' he said. 'I seem
to have twisted my ankle. I'm afraid I will not be able to walk as far as
the court. Be patient, and in a week or two I will be better, and then I
will come with you.'

His neighbour ran off and came back with his donkey. 'You can ride
my donkey,' he said. 'I will walk.'

When they arrived at the court the judge asked what their quarrel
was. 'This man has some gold coins of mine that he will not give back,'
the neighbour said. 'I have asked him, but he refuses.'

The judge turned to Nasrudin. 'What do you say to this?' he asked.

Nasrudin stood up. 'This poor neighbour of mine is a sad case,' he said. 'He has a delusion that things belong to him, when they don't. He is claiming now that my gold coins are his. I would not be surprised to hear him say that this coat that I am wearing belongs to him.'

'But it does!' shouted the neighbour.

Nasrudin approached the judge and spoke quietly to him. 'As a final test, ask him whose donkey I rode to court this morning. If he says it is his, that will prove he is deluded.'

The judge turned to the neighbour. 'You are telling me that you lent an expensive coat to this man, who already had gold coins of yours that he would not give back. I find that hard to believe. But tell me this, whose donkey is that I see outside, and who rode it here?'

'It is mine,' said the neighbour. 'It is my donkey, but I lent it to Nasrudin this morning as he had twisted his ankle.'

Nasrudin walked briskly across the court, and said, 'You see, your honour!'

The judge turned to the neighbour. 'It is not right to make false accusations against innocent citizens. You will pay Nasrudin one gold coin to make up for your evil words.'

Nasrudin smiled. 'I knew the last coin would come in the end,' he said.

The Seven Baldies and One Shorty

A STORY FROM MONGOLIA

THERE WERE SEVEN BALD MEN living in the same town. They often stayed together as they felt safer in numbers when people teased them. Some would call out, 'Hello, eggheads!' and others would cry, 'Can you see your face in your friend's head?'

One day they heard someone call out, 'Boil for four minutes and they should be good for a picnic.' That did it. The Baldies looked round to see who had shouted that—and they saw it was a very short man.

The seven Baldies were so angry they shouted, 'Come here, Shorty!' They chased the little man down the street and when they caught him

[81]

they tied him up with a rope, led him to a deserted place, and bound him to a tree.

Then they set off in seven different directions to find some ants and scorpions to bite and sting Shorty to teach him a lesson.

While Shorty was sitting helpless, tied to the tree, an elderly man, dressed in a smart blue silk coat, came along. He was riding a yellow horse, he had with him a long reed pole for catching horses, and he carried a silver tinder-box and a set of knives.

The stranger asked, 'Why are you sitting, tied to this tree?'

Shorty did not want to admit what had really happened—and he wanted to escape. So he replied, 'I am sitting here by this tree being cured of a terrible disease.'

'What sort of disease can be cured by sitting there?' asked the old man.

'I have a very bad eye-disease and this is a tree that cures diseases of the eye,' said Shorty. 'I have been sitting here for quite a long time and, look, my eyes are getting better. Have a look at my eyes. They were very bleary—are they still?'

'Your eyes are quite clear,' said the old man. 'But I have very weak eyes too. May I sit there?'

'Where are you travelling to?' asked Shorty.

'I am looking for some horses I have lost,' said the old man. 'That is why I have this reed pole for catching them.'

'I will go and look for your horses,' said Shorty. 'You come and sit here by this tree and cure your poor eyes.'

The old man untied Shorty, who dressed him in his own clothes and put on the smart silk coat. He tied the old man to the tree, picked up the silver tinder-box and the knives, mounted the yellow horse, and set off happily, pulling the reed pole behind him.

[83]

When the seven Baldies returned from their seven different directions they had collected lots of ants and scorpions. They set them loose all round Shorty, calling out, 'There you are, Shorty, that serves you right for teasing us.'

'I'm not called Shorty,' cried the old man. 'I am just sitting here to cure my eyes.'

'Nonsense,' they answered. 'We recognize your clothes. You're not going to escape like that.' So they left him fidgeting and scratching, trying to avoid the insects.

But when the Baldies got back to the town they found Shorty safe at his house, with a new horse, a reed pole, a silver tinder-box, and a set of knives, and wearing a smart coat.

'We've just come back from setting ants and scorpions on you,' they said. 'How did you get here?'

Shorty replied, 'When I was left with those insects I was bitten so much that I fainted. I went to heaven to the Water God's palace. The Water God was kindly giving everyone a new horse, a reed pole, a silk gown, a silver tinder-box, and a set of knives. When I came away there was still one beautiful white horse left, waiting for some future master. If you hurry, you may still have it.'

'Where is this place?' asked the seven Baldies eagerly.

'Follow me,' said Shorty and he led the seven Baldies to the sea. 'The first man must go into the sea with a stick. The Water God's palace is quite far into the sea, deep in the ocean. When the first one of you reaches the palace, he should wave his stick, then the rest can follow— and you will have your rewards.'

So one of the Baldies took a long walking-stick and walked into the sea. As he got in deeper he lost his footing and his stick waved in the air as he disappeared beneath the sea.

'Look, he is waving!' said Shorty. 'Go in after him! He has found the palace.'

So the remaining Baldies rushed into the sea and all disappeared beneath the waves. They thrashed about and they struggled and eventually they staggered to the shore, soaking wet and furious.

Shorty returned home to his new possessions. Soon the seven Baldies arrived home dripping wet and angry.

'Did you enjoy your swim?' cried Shorty to the Baldies. 'I may be short, and there is only one of me, but I can beat seven Baldies any day. When the eggs have dried we can have a picnic . . . Sorry! I take it all back . . . I didn't mean it . . . Oh dear, here we go again.'

The Barber's Wife

A STORY FROM INDIA

THE VILLAGE BARBER WAS HOPELESS, quite hopeless. I don't know how he ever became a barber, he was so bad. When he cut people's hair, he'd snip bits off their ears. When he shaved the men, as often as not he cut their throats. Of course, fewer and fewer people went to him until in the end he had nothing left except his razor, which he did manage to keep sharp, and his wife, who was even sharper. She was so sharp I cannot imagine how she came to marry such a hopeless barber, but she did. Don't think, though, that he was just hopeless as a barber. He was hopeless at everything.

They had become so poor that his wife was quite desperate and sent the barber to the king's palace to beg. The king was in a good mood, as it was his wedding day, and asked the barber what he would like. The silly man stood there, quite hopeless. His wife had not told him what to ask for and he really couldn't think for himself so he just mumbled, 'Oh, something, Your Majesty.'

The king smiled and offered him a piece of land, a piece suitable for a barber he said. The barber was glad not to have to answer any more questions, said thank you and left the palace. His wife rushed up to him when she saw him coming cheerfully home, expecting him to have brought some money they could use to buy bread. She was not very pleased when she heard that the king had given them a piece of land. She was even less pleased when they went to look at it and saw the most over-grown field you can imagine, just like the top of a giant's head when he hasn't been to have his hair cut for a year or two.

'What use is that to us?' she asked. 'We have no plough, no ox. Are you going to clear it with your razor?'

But the barber was pleased. 'Land is land,' he said. 'It can't run away or get lost or get stolen.'

That gave the wife her brilliant idea. She told her husband to copy everything she did, exactly. They spent the day in such an odd way that anyone less hopeless would have asked what they were doing, and that, of course, was the point.

They walked up and down the field, peering at the ground, poking sticks into the bushes, looking down the rabbit holes. When anyone came past, they sat down flop on the ground and stared up into the sky as if they were counting the birds. It was enough to make any normal person very, very curious.

Luck was on the wife's side. There was a small wood next to the field and in the small wood was a gang of seven robbers, hiding until dark. There isn't much to do when you are hiding in a wood all day and so they watched the barber and his wife and grew more and more curious until they thought they would burst from curiosity. At sunset they could stand it no longer and the chief robber walked over and asked the barber, man to man, what they were doing. He, poor man, had no idea and said so but the chief didn't believe him. Anyway, he thought it would be easier to get the truth out of a woman.

The wife put on a good act but in the end she couldn't keep a secret—What woman can? thought the robber. She told the chief robber that her grandfather had buried five pots full of gold in this field and that, now he was dead, they were going to dig them up. The trouble was, now he was dead, they didn't know where the pots were. They would have to come back tomorrow and look again. 'But you won't tell anyone, will you?' she begged him. 'It would be terrible if someone came in the night and found those five pots of gold before we did.' The chief robber swore on his honour never to tell anyone and went laughing back to his six companions and told them.

When the barber and his wife returned in the morning what had been a piece of waste ground looked like a well-ploughed field. The robbers had barely managed to crawl into the wood before collapsing, exhausted. The wife laughed all the way to the corn-dealer's shop and borrowed enough seed to sow the field. It had been so thoroughly dug that the harvest was enormous. They kept enough to feed themselves and sold the rest for a great pot full of gold coins.

When the robbers heard what had happened and realized how they had been tricked they were very angry indeed. They came to the barber's house and demanded their share of the money from the harvest. The wife laughed at them. 'I told you there was gold in the ground,' she said. 'I'm sorry you didn't find it. It's in our house now, and that's exactly where it's going to stay.'

Windy Stories

A STORY FROM THE UNITED STATES OF AMERICA

DO YOU CALL THAT A STRONG WIND? That was a faint breeze here, out west. Let me tell you what we'd call a strong wind and then you'll see that that wind wasn't even trying. It may have blown a few tiles off, but, bless you, that's what a baby wind might do when it's just learning. A real wind, now, that's quite different. Why, one day last month we had what I would call a bit of wind.

It had been a hot day and I was sitting on my back verandah, eating a plate of pie, enjoying the cool evening breeze, when this wind suddenly got up, picked me off my chair and landed me in that tree

[91]

you see there on the bank of the creek. Well, I'd kept good hold of that pie—no one can bake a pumpkin pie like my wife can—but it was kind of awkward trying to eat it at the top of the tree. So I sat and waited for the wind to die down again, and sat, and then I got a bit impatient, I will admit that, and cursed a bit. The wind must have been sorry when it heard me cursing, for I'm not usually a man who complains much. Next thing I knew, that wind had blown my shed door into the tree and wedged it down in front of me. It made a perfect table and I could finish my pie before it got cold.

While I was sitting there, what did I see but my two boys coming down the street flying kites. 'That's odd,' I said to myself. 'Surely this wind's a mite too strong for kite-flying. I hope they don't lose those kites of theirs, or get carried away. A wind that's going to pick me up and put me into this tree isn't going to have too much trouble with boys, even if there are two of them.' And then I had a good laugh for I saw that my boys had out-smarted that wind. They had taken up iron man-hole covers and were flying them as kites. They were just the right weight for that wind. You could see it was getting itself tired out tugging and tugging. Unfortunately, it had one last trick to play. As my boys had

taken the man-hole covers off, that wind crept into the drains when no one was looking and pulled out those holes and blew them right away and then it got tired and had to drop them. People were falling into holes round here for days after that.

'Course, that was just an everyday sort of wind, nothing to get too excited about. We had a pretty strong wind one time and they sent a reporter out from Kansas to write a story about it. He'd been told that old Mother Wheeler's cooking stove had been blown out of her kitchen just the day before, leaving all the pans neatly on the floor. So there he was, standing in the street, just going to talk to her when that very minute the wind came back, picked up the saucepans it had left behind and blew away with them, lids and all. He was so surprised that he opened his mouth—which he'd been warned not to do whatever happened— and whoosh! That wind got inside him and turned him completely inside out. He never did write that story.

Now, that's the worst wind I ever saw here with my own eyes, but my pa used to tell me of the days when the winds were younger and

[93]

stronger and of the tricks they played then on people. That's how he made his money, as it happens. He'd been cheated by some fast talker into buying an oil well, spent all his money on it. 'Course, there wasn't anything in that well when he came to look into it, and he was ruined. All he had left in the world was a very deep hole. That day, though, there was a bit of a blow and the wind took that oil well and blew it inside out and left it stuck there hundreds of feet into the air. So, he borrowed a saw and cut it into two-foot sections and sold it to the farmers back East for post-holes for fences.

But I was going to tell the story he told me. The worst wind he ever heard tell of hit the town next to this one, picked up every single person who was out-of-doors, blew them across country, blew them 'smack' against the wall of the town hall here—in those days it was the only brick building in the town. It blew them with such force that they were completely flattened, make a pancake look over-weight, they would. Pa and the others had to go round and peel them off. They weren't much hurt as it happened, just very, very thin. It did them a good turn as it happened. They'd been pretty poor in that town before but after that they could always earn good money working as posters and bill-boards. Talking adverts they were. You used to see them stuck up all over the county.

No, you can't call what we had last night a wind.

The Treasure Thief

A STORY FROM EGYPT

THIS IS THE STORY of how the builder's younger son became the most powerful man in Egypt after the Pharaoh himself. It wasn't luck. It took cleverness, but not just cleverness alone. It also took wickedness, and conceit. Oh, and it took trust in another's word as well. Without any one of them the builder's younger son would still have been a builder, or worse. Much worse. Dead. Or worse than dead.

The story starts with money, with piles and piles and piles of silver. The Pharaoh had so much silver that he needed a new Treasure House to keep it safe. Like everyone with more money than they can spend he worried about other people getting their hands on it. So, he sent for his Master Builder and ordered him to build a new Treasure House so strong

[95]

that no one would be able to break in and with a door lock so secret that only the Pharaoh himself would be able to open it.

The Master Builder stood in front of the Pharaoh and listened to his orders. The Pharaoh's little son was playing at his father's feet. The Master Builder watched and thought of the enormous piles of silver this little boy would inherit when his father died. He thought of his own two sons at home and of what they would inherit: his bag of tools and perhaps a few silver coins, if they were lucky. A clever idea crept into his mind and would not go away.

The new Treasure House was built, the safest building there had ever been in the land of Egypt. The Pharaoh was pleased, and grew steadily richer. The Master Builder was praised, and stayed poor.

Time passed and the Master Builder grew old, and sick, and at last knew that he was dying. He called his two sons to him, now grown men, and builders like their father. 'I have nothing to leave you from the labour of my hands.' He held up his hands, scarred and worn from his life of building in stone. 'I have nothing to leave you, except the care of your mother.'

Well, the two brothers were good sons. They promised their father that they would care for their mother, swore on all the gods they would work for her and care for her. Then the Master Builder smiled and told them the secret he had carried all these years. 'I have riches to leave you from the work of my mind,' he said. While they stared at him in silent wonder he told them of the Treasure House he had built for the Pharaoh when they were little children. He told them that he had cunningly set a stone that could be moved in the outer wall, and told them where to find it and how to move it.

After their father died times became hard and the family poor. One moonless night the two brothers crept to the wall of the Treasure House, found the stone their father had told them of, pushed it in the way he had told them, and crept into the darkness. Here they felt the great barrels filled with silver coins and put handful after handful into the bags they had brought with them. They crept out, replaced the stone and went home.

The Pharaoh had become more and more miserly as his treasure had grown. He liked to go into his Treasure House every morning early to run his fingers through his piles of silver. He could not count it, there was too much, far too much, but he knew it all by feel. That morning he knew at once that some had gone. But how? There was no hole in the wall, no tunnel through the floor, no sky hole in the roof. The door had been sealed as only he knew how to seal it.

Of course, the brothers did not go only once but again and again and again. The Pharaoh became desperate. Finally, he ordered traps to be set among his barrels of silver, vicious traps that would hold a man and never let him go. When the traps were set, he closed the door carefully and waited for morning.

By now the two brothers knew the Treasure House well. They had never used a light on their thieving trips because they feared that it might give them away. The elder brother went first, moved confidently towards the nearest barrel, when . . .

His cry would have brought all the guards running if the walls had not been so thick. His younger brother froze with shock half-way into the chamber, and it's lucky that he did. 'Fetch light!' his brother ordered him. 'Do not, whatever you do, take one step into here. Hurry!'

The brother did as he was told. He ran home as fast as he could, snatched up a light, ran back, and crawled into the Treasure House and

saw it for the first time, and saw his brother held fast in the claws of the trap. Alas, the trap-maker knew his job too well. Struggle all they could, there was no way they could open the claws and release the prisoner. They stared at each other in dismay as the first cock-crows of the new day rang out.

'Cut off my head,' said the trapped brother. 'Cut off my head and take it away and bury it. If you do that you and our mother will be safe. If you do not, we will all die slowly and horribly.'

This is the wicked thing the younger brother had to do, for it *is* a wicked thing to kill your brother, even if it is the only thing that you *can* do. He had to do it, and he did it, and it was a wicked act.

The Pharaoh came early to his Treasure House that day. The door was sealed with his own seal. The walls were whole, the floor was smooth, the roof was solid still. But! There, inside this sealed room, was a headless body in his trap. A headless body! And, what was worse, less silver than there had been the day before. (The younger brother knew he could never return and had carried away as much as he could, as well as his brother's head.) The Pharaoh was furious, he was amazed, but he was also crafty. He ordered the body to be taken out of the trap and hung up outside the gate of the palace. He ordered soldiers to guard it and to report anyone who seemed distressed.

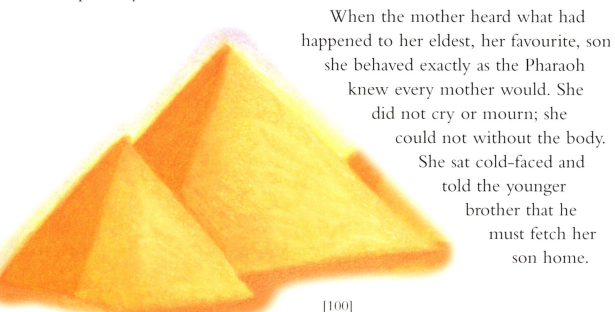

When the mother heard what had happened to her eldest, her favourite, son she behaved exactly as the Pharaoh knew every mother would. She did not cry or mourn; she could not without the body. She sat cold-faced and told the younger brother that he must fetch her son home.

In vain he explained to her what would happen if he tried. She sat in terrible stillness and said quietly, 'Bring him home.'

Cleverness at last came to his rescue and he knew what to do. He borrowed five donkeys, he bought ten leather bags full of wine, he tied the bags cunningly on the donkeys, he set off that evening for the palace gate. When he was opposite the soldiers he gave a twitch of the ropes and three of the wine bags tipped and started to spill their wine on the ground. He panicked and ran from donkey to donkey, shouting and trying to stop the flow, but whatever he did just seemed to make things worse. The guards rushed over with their water bottles and tried to help him but, no matter what they did, the wine would somehow end up inside their water bottles.

At last the three bags were empty and the younger brother stood, wiping his forehead. He was so grateful to the guards for their help, for their trying to help at least, that he insisted on giving them a whole, a new, bag bulging full of wine. The guards, by now extremely cheerful, insisted on him joining them in drinking it. One bag led inevitably to a second and by the time darkness had fallen, so had the guards. All lay snoring open-mouthed. The younger brother stood up, suddenly quite sober, and cut down his brother's body, and loaded it upon one of the donkeys. Before he left he shaved the beard from the right cheek of each of the guards.

This shaving was the first sign of the conceit that was so important for the next part. For the story could end here, with the mother and her son living happily ever after on all the silver he had taken from the Treasure House and the head and body of the elder quietly buried. But it didn't, because of his conceit.

The Pharaoh was so enraged at the trick that had been played on him, at the way he had been made a joke throughout the city, that he swore he would catch the criminal, and used his only daughter as the bait. He made her sit in the gate to the palace every evening and he said that she would marry the man who told her the cleverest and the wickedest thing he had done. If anyone told her the story of the theft of the body she was to grab his arm and yell and the guards would rush out from hiding and seize the man.

The younger brother could not resist; his conceit was too great. He wrapped himself in a thick cloak and set off to the palace. On the way he passed the hospital and went in for a moment. When the Pharaoh's daughter asked him what was the wickedest thing he had ever done, he said, 'I cut off my brother's head.' When she asked him, trembling a little with excitement for she guessed what the answer would be, what was the cleverest, he said, 'Rescuing his body from the guards.'

At once she grabbed the hand stretched out towards her and held on tight and yelled and yelled for the guards. As they rushed out with their lanterns and torches a strange sight met them. The Pharaoh's daughter sat holding a hand. The hand was attached to an arm all right, but the arm itself was attached to . . . nothing. The younger brother had cut off the arm from a man who had died in the hospital and had held it out under cover of his cloak and of the darkness as he guessed the trap that had been set for him.

Trust in another's word, I said. The Pharaoh was a great ruler, even if he was a miserly man, and he recognized the brilliance of the younger brother. He made a proclamation that the Treasure Thief could marry his daughter and become Pharaoh's chief minister, if he came forward. The younger brother did trust the Pharaoh's word and did come to the palace, not quite sure if it would be to his death. He did marry the daughter. He was a wise chief minister, and they did then all live happily ever after.

The Blind Man, the Lame Man, and the Hunchback

A STORY FROM NEPAL

THREE FRIENDS, one blind, one lame, and one hunchbacked, had to beg from door to door to make a living. They were very poor and would pick up what they could from neighbours and from rubbish tips. One day, as they were on their daily round, they found a pointed iron spike, a chisel, and a hammer.

'I could use an iron spike, I'm sure,' said the blind man.

'I could use a chisel too,' said the lame man.

'That hammer will come in useful,' said the hunchback.

[105]

They were all very excited by their new finds, and brought them home and put them aside for when they might come in useful.

'I think these tools could bring us luck,' said the blind man. 'Let us move away from here and try our fortunes in a different place.'

The other two agreed with him. They took some food with them and their new-found tools, and set off. As they travelled they found a goat by the roadside, so they decided to take that with them too.

They soon came to the edge of a forest. As they had never moved away from their town before they had never been in a forest and were frightened about what might live there.

They entered the forest very cautiously and soon came to a huge building. It looked like some sort of palace but it was so big that it could not belong to ordinary humans.

The lame man said, 'There may be someone in there who can help us. It looks as if whoever it is can afford to do so—they must be very rich.'

They entered the palace and to their surprise they found there was no one to greet them or to tell them to go away. It seemed completely empty. So they shut and bolted the door from the inside and went upstairs to the third floor, where they tied up the goat in a corner and left it bleating.

In fact this palace belonged to a cruel giant who used to wander round the countryside stealing from his neighbours. That is what he was doing at that moment. When he returned to his home he was surprised to find his palace locked and bolted from the inside. He roared out in a thunderous voice, 'Who is there inside my palace?'

He listened for an answer but the only sound he heard in reply was the bleating of the goat. He had never

heard this sort of noise before and he started to become worried and frightened. He could not imagine what was inside his palace.

'What sort of person are you,' he shouted, 'that makes such a strange sound?' And he thrust one of his fingers through the peephole in the door to see if he could feel anything.

The three friends were keeping very quiet inside the palace, but they were terrified by the angry sound of the giant's voice. As soon as they saw his finger poking through the hole they took up the pointed iron spike and pricked his finger with it. The giant gave a loud cry of pain and quickly removed his finger from the door.

'I warn you,' shouted the giant, 'I am much bigger than you. Let me show you the size of my hand.' And he forced his whole hand through the letter box. The three friends took up their hammer and aimed a mighty blow at the giant's hand. The giant gave another cry of pain.

[107]

'Very well,' he cried. 'I am now going to see what sort of people you are,' and he put his eye to the peep-hole in the door. But the three friends took the chisel and poked his eye with it so that he was blinded in one eye.

Then the giant ran away, certain that the people in his palace were no ordinary humans. He hurried off to his giant friends nearby.

'There is a mysterious creature in my palace,' he exclaimed. 'It makes a noise I have never heard before, it has sharp claws, and can hit very hard.'

A giantess spoke up first. 'Leave this to me,' she said. 'I'll soon see what this creature is.' But she too came away with a sore finger, a very sore hand, and a very, very sore eye.

'Come on,' she said to all the giants. 'We must climb the walls of the palace and see what is inside.'

Meanwhile, the three friends were getting hungry. So they explored the kitchen in the giant's palace and found piles of delicious food and prepared quite a feast for themselves. They spread it all out on the long table in the giant's hall.

Several giants now approached the palace and decided to form a ladder of giants in order to see in at the top floor. The giant who owned the palace, and who had already suffered at the hands of the three friends, offered to be the one to stand on the ground—others could climb on top and look in. He reckoned he would be safer that way.

Soon the giants formed a ladder and the one at the top looked in at the window. To his surprise, instead of the super-beings he was expecting, he saw just three ordinary humans sitting down to a feast. He was about to call down that they were just three ordinary humans—the sort that giants usually ate themselves—when one of the friends, looking at the feast spread out from one end of the long table to the other, said, 'Which end should we begin eating—the upper end or the lower end?'

'The lower end,' shouted the blind man.

The giant at the bottom of the ladder heard this and he thought he was going to be eaten first. He was so frightened that he began to shake himself free—he wanted to run away into the forest.

When the bottom of the giant-ladder went away all the rest of the ladder collapsed. The three friends heard a terrific crash outside the window. When they looked out they were amazed to see a heap of giants all moaning and bellowing in pain.

While the giants were struggling to get up and run away, the three friends helped themselves to the treasure that the giant had in his palace—which had, of course, been stolen from the people round about—and ran off home before the giants could discover just how harmless they really were. They took some of the treasure themselves and returned the rest to the grateful neighbours.

'You never know when an iron spike will come in handy,' said the blind man.

'Or a chisel,' said the lame man.

'Or a hammer,' said the hunchback.

'Or a goat,' said all three together.

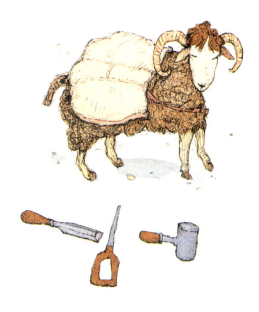

Momotaro the Peach Boy

A STORY FROM JAPAN

'IF ONLY WE HAD A SON to help us in the fields,' said the old man one day.

The old man lived with his wife out in the country. They worked hard on the land and lived a simple life. Every day the old man used to cut grass for the farmers round about and his wife kept the house and worked in their own little rice field.

One day the old man went off to cut grass as usual and the old woman took some washing down to the river. As she was washing the clothes she looked up and was very surprised to see a huge peach floating down the river towards her. She had never seen a peach so big before and she was determined to take it back to her husband. With a stick she managed to bring the peach nearer, and she picked it out of the water and carried it home.

When the old man came home after a hard day's work in the fields his wife said to him, 'I have a nice surprise for your supper. Look!'

When the old man saw the peach he exclaimed, 'I have never seen such a big peach. Where did you buy it?'

'I didn't buy it. It floated down the river and I brought it home.'

'Let us cut it now, as I am both hungry and thirsty,' said the old man; and he went to fetch the kitchen knife.

But just as he was about to cut the peach in half, it moved on the table. Then, to their astonishment, the peach split itself in half and out came a little child.

When they had got over their surprise the old man and the old woman were very excited.

'Here is the son we have always wanted,' said the old woman. And they decided they would bring the child up as their own. They gave him a bowl of rice which he ate up at once, and gradually they made plans to take care of him as he grew up. They called him Momotaro—which means 'son of a peach'.

But there was only one problem. Momotaro would not talk. The old man and the old woman wanted so much to play with their new son and to talk with him. But when the old woman tried to tickle him and play he would not make a sound. When the old man tried to play 'pat-a-cake' he just turned away and yawned.

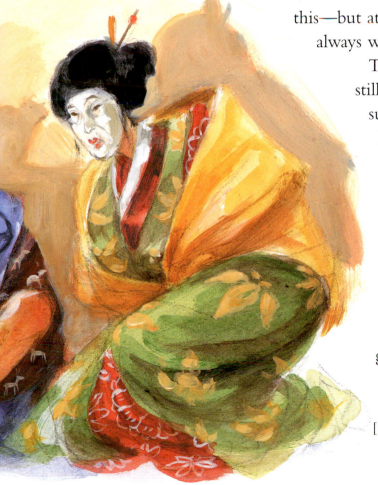

The old man and the old woman were very sad at this—but at least they had the son they had always wished for.

Time passed and Momotaro grew—but still he did not say anything. Then suddenly, when Momotaro was fifteen, he spoke. But what he said did not please the old couple very much. He said, 'I must go away now.'

The old couple were heartbroken.

'But why do you want to leave us?' asked the old man. 'We waited so long for a son and now you want to leave us. We have given you a good home and you have been happy. Where will you go?'

[113]

'You have certainly been very
good to me and made me happy,'
replied Momotaro. 'But if you let me
go now I promise I shall return.'

'Why do you want to go—and where?'
asked the old woman sadly.

'I am Momotaro,' said the boy. 'It is my duty to defeat
the band of devils that live on an island not far from here. They come
and attack villages, they steal, and they set fire to houses. I, Momotaro,
must go and conquer these devils and return what they have stolen.
Then I promise I shall return home to you.'

There was nothing the old man and the old woman could do to
make him change his mind. So the old man prepared him a suit of
clothes and the old woman made him some rice dumplings for his
journey—and off went Momotaro.

After he had travelled some way Momotaro felt hungry, so he sat
down by the roadside and began to eat one of the rice dumplings.
Suddenly a huge dog jumped out from the tall grass.

'Who are you, passing by my field without permission? Give me all
those rice dumplings or I shall bite you.'

'I am Momotaro and I am on my way to fight the devils,' Momotaro
replied. 'Come with me—your bark and your bite can help me greatly.'

'I will go with you to fight the devils,' said the dog. 'But first—can I
have just one dumpling?'

'Here you are,' said Momotaro, and they set off together.

For some time they walked over the hills and through the valleys.
Suddenly, as they were passing through a wood, a monkey dropped down
from a tree.

'Who do you think you are, coming through my woods?' asked the
monkey cheekily.

'I am Momotaro and I am on my way to fight the devils.
You can come too, if you like—you can climb up to and into places

that we cannot reach.'

'You don't need a silly monkey to join you,' said the dog. 'Let's go on.'

'Who are you calling a silly monkey?' shouted the monkey.

And the dog and the monkey began to fight, as dogs and monkeys are always enemies.

'Stop fighting!' shouted Momotaro. 'If the monkey is brave enough to come with us, we can certainly use his help.' So the monkey was given one of the rice dumplings and the three set off together.

Soon they came to a large field, and a beautiful bird flew down and stood in the field in front of them. The bird had feathers of five different colours and on its head it had a bright red cap. The dog at once tried to attack it but the bird struck out with the spurs on its feet.

Momotaro seized the dog and pulled it off the bird.

'Why are you blocking our path?' he asked the bird. 'Surely you do not want a fight?'

'I just wanted to know who you were, coming through my field,' the bird replied.

'I am Momotaro and I am off to defeat the devils. Would you come with us? You can fly to places we cannot reach.'

'I will come along—as long as your friend the dog does not attack me again.'

'Very well, come with us. Here is a rice dumpling for you before we set off.'

A dog, a monkey, and a pheasant made an unlikely group; but Momotaro told them they were not to fight each other but all were to fight the devils. So all three followed Momotaro calmly and peacefully.

At last they came to the sea, and Momotaro put them all into a small boat. At first the dog, the monkey, and the pheasant were very scared of the rocking and tossing of the boat. But they soon became used to it and they each took turns looking out from the boat

for the first sight of the island.

Soon they saw it. On the top of a steep cliff was a great castle on a rock jutting out to sea—this was the devils' stronghold. At once Momotaro said to the pheasant, 'Now we can use your flying. Fly over that castle and see what the devils are doing.'

So the pheasant flew to the top part of the castle and soon saw that the devils were having some sort of celebration and feast. He immediately flew back to tell Momotaro.

'Now is just the time to take them by surprise,' Momotaro said, and they beached the boat and clambered up to the main gate of the castle. It would not open.

Momotaro said to the monkey, 'Now we can use your climbing. Climb over and release the gate from the other side.'

'Leave this to me,' said the monkey. He quickly managed to climb over the gate and release the latch from the inside. Then Momotaro, the dog, the monkey, and the pheasant flung open the gate and went inside.

The devils were so occupied in feasting and celebrating that they were taken completely by surprise.

Momotaro said to the dog, 'Now we can use your bark and your bite.' Soon there was great confusion. The pheasant attacked the devils from above and the monkey slipped in and out among them, biting and scratching them as he went. They were terrified of the dog's bark and of its bites; and Momotaro himself, with more strength than a human, soon had them throwing themselves off the clifftop into the sea.

The chief of the devils soon gave in. Momotaro made him promise to give up his evil ways and to leave the people on the mainland in peace. The chief agreed and the devils filled the boat with treasures and then lined up, bowing, as the dog, the monkey, the pheasant, and Momotaro went back on board ship.

'Allow me to help you,' said the chief. And he took a deep breath and blew the boat on its way to the mainland.

The whole country gave the hero Momotaro and his three companions a great welcome when they returned to the mainland. And Momotaro kept his promise and returned to the old man and the old woman.

They were overjoyed to see Momotaro again. They had been so happy when he was with them and had missed him greatly while he had been away. He gave them the treasure from the island of the devils so they were able to live well as a reward for looking after the hero, Momotaro, when he was young. The dog, the monkey, and the pheasant returned to the long grass, the trees, and the fields—and they never fought with each other again.

The Monkey and the Buddha

A STORY FROM CHINA

THE MONKEY HAD MANY MAGIC POWERS but he often used them for monkey-tricks.

This monkey had been hatched from an egg that was lying on the peak of a high mountain. When the wind blew softly across the peak the baby monkey was born. The gods realized from his mysterious birth that this was a very special monkey. They gave him many magic powers—he could fly through the air and could turn into seventy-two different shapes. So no one could harm him—or even punish him if he was naughty.

[119]

But the monkey became so proud of his powers, and showed off so much, that the gods became angry with him. In the end, when the monkey said, 'With all my powers I should be the ruler of heaven,' they brought him before the emperor of the gods.

But the emperor did not know what to do. He could not control a monkey who had such powers. In the end he sent for the Buddha.

'My Lord Buddha,' said the emperor, 'this monkey is impossible to control and now says that he should be the ruler of heaven.'

The monkey was called before the Buddha.

'I understand that you wish to rule heaven,' said the Buddha. 'Why do you wish that?'

'I know that I am powerful enough to rule heaven,' replied the monkey.

'And how can you prove that you are so powerful?' asked the Buddha.

'I am going to live for ever; no one can hurt me; I can change into seventy-two different shapes; I can fly through the air; and I can jump across the world,' boasted the monkey.

The Buddha did not think it likely that the monkey could jump even out of the Buddha's palm. But he decided to teach this monkey a lesson. So he said to the monkey, 'You must show me your powers. If you can do as you say you can, you should certainly be allowed to rule heaven.'

The monkey was very excited. He practised jumping across seas and across whole countries, and finally he leapt into the air and jumped across heaven and landed at the furthest point of the earth. He found himself at the base of a great mountain. He wrote his name on one of the rocks on the mountain and then leapt straight back to the Buddha.

'There you are,' he said. 'I have jumped across heaven, written my name on a mountain at the other side of the earth, and I have jumped back here. Doesn't that prove my powers?'

But the Buddha laughed at the monkey, who believed that he had crossed the earth with a single bound, and he showed him the mountain where he had written his name. It was the base of one of the Buddha's own fingers—the monkey had not even escaped from the Buddha's hand.

Then the Buddha closed his hand and kept the monkey inside his grasp for a hundred years—to teach him a lesson.

The Story of Da Trang
and the Pearl

A STORY FROM VIETNAM

DA TRANG WAS A HUNTER who lived on the outskirts of
the forest. Every morning he would leave his thatched hut, go
into the forest with his bow and arrows, and hunt for anything
he could find.

One day on his way to his hunting he passed a temple and there he
saw two small dark snakes, with white spots, lying in the sun. Many
people would have been afraid at first because such snakes are dangerous.
But Da Trang knew that these were holy snakes, sacred to the temple.
They did him no harm and soon he would pass them every day quite

[123]

happily. He even began to take small pieces of meat from the animals he had shot to leave for the snakes.

One day when Da Trang was passing the temple he heard a strange noise, and when he looked closer he saw his two spotted snakes being attacked by a huge serpent. Da Trang fired an arrow at the serpent. He hit it and wounded it, so that it slithered away. One of the dark snakes went after it but the other was dead. Da Trang buried the dead snake behind the temple.

That night a genie came to Da Trang and said, 'You not only saved my life but in your kindness you buried my wife honourably. I am very grateful and I have a gift for you.'

Suddenly the genie turned into a snake. It opened its mouth and out fell a beautiful white pearl.

Da Trang had heard that if you possessed a pearl from a snake-genie you could understand the language of the animals, so he decided to try

this out. The next day as he set off hunting in the forest he put the pearl in his mouth.

As soon as he entered the forest he heard a voice which seemed to come from a tree.

'Two hundred paces to your right—do you see a deer? Two hundred paces to your right—do you see a deer?'

It was the voice of a crow. Da Trang took two hundred paces to his right—and there was a deer. He shot it and as he stooped to pick it up the voice said, 'Don't forget my reward. Don't forget my reward.'

'What do you want for your reward?' asked Da Trang.

'Just the insides, just the insides,' came the reply. So Da Trang cut up the deer and gave the entrails to the crow. The next day and for days to come Da Trang left meat for the crow in the same place and each day the crow showed him where to find animals to hunt.

One day the crow's meat was stolen. The crow came to complain, but Da Trang became angry and fired a poisoned arrow at it. He missed, but the crow flew to where the arrow had landed, picked it up in his beak and flew off crying, 'Revenge! Revenge!'

After a while Da Trang thought no more about this. But several days later his poisoned arrow was found in the body of a man who had recently drowned. Officers came to arrest Da Trang. He shouted that he was innocent but he was put into gaol.

One day the gaoler was surprised to hear Da Trang apparently laughing and talking to himself.

When he realized that Da Trang was in fact talking to the insects in his cell, he thought he was mad. Da Trang would ask the mosquitoes not to bite him and then they would tell him which prisoners were better to bite and which were very tough.

Once Da Trang heard some sparrows boasting to each other how they had been stealing grain from the royal granaries and how easy this was as they were so poorly guarded. Da Trang told the prison warden. He did not believe him at first but later found that what he said was true and he told the king.

Later Da Trang saw some ants hurriedly carrying their eggs and food to higher ground. He asked them why they were in such a hurry, and they told him that there was soon going to be a flood. Da Trang once again told the warden, who told the king. The king ordered his men to make preparations in case of a flood—and three days later the river rose and overflowed and flooded large areas of the kingdom.

So the king called Da Trang to the palace and asked him how he knew of these things. Da Trang told him the story of the crow and of the snakes, and of how he had acquired the pearl. Then he showed the king his pearl.

The king was an honest man and, although he realized how much could be done with this pearl, he did not take it from Da Trang but kept asking him all he heard from the animals. Soon Da Trang was able to show the king that animals, like humans, have their own worlds and their own feelings and behave much as humans do.

The king took Da Trang for long walks by the sea and Da Trang talked with many kinds of fish. They often went out on a boat on the sea, and one day, while Da Trang was resting on the boat in the sunshine and the king was watching the dolphins playing in the sea, there was suddenly a strange sound. Da Trang, looking over the side, saw a cuttlefish swimming along beside the king's boat, singing. He laughed out loud—and the pearl fell out of his mouth and into the sea.

Da Trang was desperate. The king marked the spot where the pearl fell in and divers were sent down to find it—but all in vain. The pearl was gone.

The king soon turned his thoughts to other matters but Da Trang was so shattered that he thought about the lost pearl all the time.

The king continued to treat him well but Da Trang would not be comforted. He was so broken-hearted that soon he became mad. To take revenge on the sea for taking his pearl he decided to fill it up with sand so that it would no longer exist. He gathered many workmen to bring hundreds of cartloads of sand to the seashore. At first the king allowed him to do this as he felt sorry for him, but in the end the workmen stopped as they saw that poor Da Trang was truly mad.

The workmen had made a huge pile of sand on the seashore. Now all Da Trang could do was to sit and watch the sea gradually swallow up the sand—just as it had swallowed up his precious magic pearl.

The Two Kings

A STORY FROM WEST AFRICA

TWO KINGS, TWO GREAT KINGS. Let us start with
Sumanguru. He was a king indeed: tall, handsome, with eyes
that looked into the very corners of your mind, and a great
warrior. Proud, of course, as a great king should be, shouldn't he?

Yes, Sumanguru was a proud king. One day he heard that the King of
Tabon was passing through his kingdom, going to the city of Niani, and
he sent a messenger inviting him to rest and eat. The messenger returned,
alone, terrified, and fell before Sumanguru. The king stretched out, held
the man's chin in his hand, and stared into his eyes. 'Tell me what he said.'

[129]

The messenger forgot the polite lies he had made up on his journey back to Sosso and found his mouth spilling out the truth, always a dangerous thing to tell a king. '"Who is Sumanguru?" he said, Master. "Tell whoever he is that I go to visit a real king, a king who rules a real kingdom wisely, a king who fears God. The King of Niani." These were the words of the King of Tabon, and his people laughed, Master.'

Sumanguru flung the messenger from him and left the palace and shouted for his horse and cursed his grooms and guards when they tried to ride with him. He galloped until he was out of sight of his city and then sat under a tree, cursing still. Now he cursed his own kingdom for being too small. He cursed the King of Tabon for his slighting words. He cursed the King of Niani for his lands and for his love of God, and, so hurt in his pride was he, he cursed God too for giving fame to his servant.

As Sumanguru cursed God a stone in front of him swelled, twitched, and two red eyes opened and looked at Sumanguru. A bent and splintery arm broke out of the stone and pointed a finger at the king. A mouth opened and a voice spoke, a voice like the grinding of pebbles on a beach.

'You called. I came.'

'I did not call you,' Sumanguru said. Although he was a great and proud king, a little fear stirred in his heart.

'You cursed my enemy,' ground out the voice of the stone, 'and that makes you my friend.'

'How could you be my friend?' Sumanguru asked, fear leaving him.

'I know your thoughts, Great King. I know that all your people fear you, yet you must shelter from the midday sun. I know your people give you gold, but if the rain gives you nothing all will die. I know you stride your kingdom and all fall back, but the wind makes you stagger. I know you think you are nothing: weaker than the sun, less important than the rain, less stubborn than the wind.'

Sumanguru said nothing, for these were indeed the thoughts that wormed inside him in the night. The voice ground on. 'I can tell you the future too. I can see a sorcerer king sitting on a throne with all the kings that man has ever heard of subject to him.'

'Who is that man?'

The stone turned slowly towards the mountain. As it turned its voice said, 'That king of kings is the man brave enough to follow me into the mountains.'

Sumanguru got to his feet, held his horse by its bridle and walked after the stone into the great mountains. There he made a pact with the demons of the earth. He would fight with their power against all the kings who served God. They made him safe from all dangers, except one, for no man can be immortal. The only thing on earth that could harm him now was the spur from a rooster's foot.

He returned to Sosso and ordered all the roosters to be destroyed and then he took his army and conquered all the lands as far as he could march, starting with Tabon whose king had insulted him. No one could stand against him. The very earth itself seemed to fight with him.

This is the first king, the first great king.

The second king was born now, born in the troubled city of Niani, born the twelfth son of its good king.

His brothers were all strong, fine men like their father. He wasn't. All babies crawl. He went on crawling, could not stand like a man. His legs would not hold him up but dragged useless behind him in the dust. He kept his mouth shut against the dust and never spoke. He was ugly, like a frog. And as he grew, he became a thief. The women of the city called him Sundiata, which means the Lion of Thieves, the King of Thieves—and that was the only kingdom he was likely to have, after all, with eleven fine brothers. He could never be King of Niani.

Sumanguru made sure he was. Every year he rode into the city and summoned the king. Every year he took the fairest children as slaves, the best of the harvest as tax. Every year he raised his hand, and the king fell slain at his feet. Eleven years, eleven kings. As the eleventh brother lay bleeding into the earth Sumanguru laughed. 'Where is your king now? Bring him out that I may greet him.'

Sundiata crawled across, dusty, ugly, and raised himself on his hands. 'I am king now,' he said, and they were the first words he had spoken.

'Stand before me,' sneered Sumanguru, 'for I am king of kings and I command you.'

'I will stand,' said Sundiata, 'but I need a stick. My legs are weak.'

Sumanguru gestured and a guard brought a stick. Sundiata struggled to stand but the stick broke as he leant his weight on it. 'Fetch this fat slug a bar of iron,' Sumanguru ordered. 'He is too heavy for mere wood.'

[133]

A rod of iron was brought and it twisted and bent as Sundiata tried
to stand. 'Bring me the royal sceptre,' he said, panting in the dust.
Everyone laughed as the royal sceptre was placed in his hands, the thin
cane with its silver knob. A child could have broken it—snap!—across
one knee. Sundiata took it in his hand and stood. He faced Sumanguru,
who laughed.

'Party tricks,' he said. 'Enjoy your year as king,' and turned his horse
and rode away, a little uneasy in his heart. The two kings had met for the
first time. They would meet three times, but at their second meeting
Sumanguru did not recognize Sundiata, for he came, like a thief, in
disguise and stole the most precious thing he had, his secret.

A singer came to Sosso and drew crowds. His fame spread into
the palace and Sumanguru called him to sing to him. The song was
all in praise of the great deeds of the great sorcerer king and it was

sweet to the king's ears. He called for more but the singer threw himself at his feet. 'I dare not,' he said. 'The words of songs have their own magic and are dangerous. If, by chance, I sang of what could harm you, I fear what might happen. I spent many hours on the song I sang you checking that nothing in it had ever done you harm. I have written a song of your greater glories to come but dare not sing it out loud. Excuse me, lord.'

Sumanguru stood and led the singer into a quiet corner. 'Tell me,' he said, 'are there hens or roosters in your song?'

The singer nodded, seemed more worried, and, at last, learned, under many oaths of secrecy, the king's weak point: if he were wounded by a rooster's spur all his sorcerer's powers would drain away and he would be just a man. The singer smiled and sang, and sang, and next morning was nowhere to be found.

[135]

Twelve months had passed since Sundiata first stood up as king and Sumanguru and his men rode into Niani to collect slaves and food, and to kill the king. Sundiata stood, waiting. He did not lean on the royal sceptre but had a light spear in his hand. No children had been collected; no food was piled ready.

Sumanguru's eyes flashed but before he could signal to his guards the spear in Sundiata's hand flashed too and struck his shoulder. As the king pulled it out he saw with horror that it was tipped with a rooster's spur, and he knew he was doomed. He turned his horse, and fled. Mocking laughter followed him.

As he galloped a cavern opened up in front of him and he pulled his horse sharply back. A stone in front of him swelled, twitched, and two red eyes opened and looked at Sumanguru. A bent and splintery arm broke out of the stone and pointed a finger at the king. A mouth opened and a voice spoke, a voice like the grinding of pebbles on a beach. 'Welcome, king of kings!' he said, and he led Sumanguru into the land of demons under the earth.

Maria the Tall

A STORY FROM COLOMBIA

I RECKON IT WAS MARIA THE TALL who took him away. We had just gone out to cut wood, my friend and I. My wife warned me: 'Don't go to the ravine, and be back by nightfall.' But I took no notice—she has a lot of silly fears.

No one can beat my friend at talking. Not for anything. Not even if you paid someone for each word.

They say that before she appears you hear something like a whistle—like the sound the wind makes when it slips itself through the crack in a window.

But I heard nothing at all; nor did my friend, because he hadn't drawn breath while talking.

We piled up the firewood we had cut to make it easier to carry. I have to confess that going for a swim in the ravine was my idea. It was just that we were so close to it, and it was such a hot day . . . As nobody likes to venture there the place is all clean, fresh, and unspoilt. I have never seen such green ferns and brightly coloured grasses, nor water so clear. A sweet yet sharp fragrance filled the air, like that perfume that girls wear on Sundays when they go out in search of a man.

When my friend came out of the water his eyes were open wide, and they were fixed on something between the trees. I followed the direction of his gaze—and I saw a beautiful young woman begin to appear. Only in fairy stories are there women like this one, I swear. Her black, swirling hair was settling over her shoulders, her dark eyes were staring—at us.

My friend was moving towards her. Realizing that she was some apparition I shouted at him to keep back. He did not hear, or did not want to hear. The woman smiled a mocking smile, then let out a laugh that entranced him. He continued towards her. I wanted to run to keep close behind my friend, but a mysterious force compelled me to stay still.

He followed the woman, as if in a trance. She was now moving towards the mountain area, leading him on. And I just stood there, unable to move, unable to do anything.

I do not know how much time passed, but when I found that I could move again the sun had just gone down. I looked back to where I saw them disappear. I have never felt such heat. The heavy, humid air hardly allowed me to breathe. There was not a sound. It was as if life had ceased.

I noticed the same fragrance as before and, like a dog following a scent, I followed the trail. I turned to the left. The scent became stronger, it became unbearable. I felt sick—and then the ghostly figure of

a woman appeared. She was no longer the beautiful woman that my friend had followed. She was devilish now—her eyes seemed to pour out fire and her laugh sounded like the flapping of wings.

I tried to reach her to ask for my friend, but as I touched her she started to become taller and taller—until she became only a shadow that grew and grew and grew.

That is all I know. Of my friend—nothing. But I have to keep looking for him. I must.

Notes on the Stories

Anansi and the Banana Bird

Many years ago men and women were taken from their country in West Africa to America, where they were sold as slaves. They were made to work hard under the hot sun, and were often beaten and insulted if they rested for a minute. So at the end of a day's work they would gather round and tell stories to keep their spirits up—stories such as this one.

There are many stories of Anansi. When the children see a spider, they know it is that cunning creature, Anansi. I am grateful to Irene Vasco for assistance with source material and to Nick Paleocrassas for help with translation. (CS-C)

The Two Cats

This story was told to me by someone who swears it is true and happened in Ireland. He's an honest man. (MH)

Robin Hood and Sir Richard Lee

Stories of Robin Hood in England go back at least six hundred years. I have taken one of the earliest known ballads and retold the first part of it to make it a story about telling stories. (MH)

The Fox and the Tomten

This story from Sweden combines two familiar figures in folk tales in many countries. The fox appears frequently, as it is a familiar animal and one associated with cunning—which can lead to good stories. The Tomten is an imaginary dwarf-like figure (rather like an Irish leprechaun) who provides the unusual image. The scenery and the weather are very Swedish and so make the story belong more obviously to that part of the world, the frozen North. (CS-C)

The Frog Princess

The character of a frog-princess is very popular in stories in many parts of the world. We have chosen to include one from Italy and one from Russia. This version from Russia has many Russian elements—the tsar, forests, 'I smell a Russian', and typical Russian scenery—but also many features that occur in different versions of the story.

I am grateful to Julie Voropayeva and Maria Chernyakova for help over source material. I met them in England and asked them to send me a Russian story when they returned home. They went their separate ways and both sent me the same story—so it is obviously a popular one. (CS-C)

The Three Wives

I have changed this Italian version of the frog-princess story slightly because, as a middle child myself, I grew very tired of the youngest son always winning. I have also made the middle son a reader of stories. I was too, but I didn't kiss any frogs. I didn't have to, luckily. (MH)

Flood

This story comes from the Inca people of the high Andes mountains of South America and celebrates the fact that these lands are near the sky and far above the earth's floor. It's one of many flood stories from all around the world (see our book *Noah's Ark* for more). I have freely adapted the story from accounts in various books I have read on the Incas. If you're worried about the colour of the fox's tail on page 44, there's a different fox there. These have black tips to their tails instead of the white tips that English foxes have. (MH)

Water

This story is one that the Native Americans on the north-west coast told. Their stories were about Raven, who was their particular animal-god, as the Plains Indians' stories were about Coyote, and in South Eastern America about Hare or Rabbit. There is a longer version of this story, and more stories of Raven, in *Raven the Trickster* by Gail Robinson. (MH)

The Star-Wife

I have adapted this story from several similar South American ones I found. Is it too sad? Although it doesn't have a traditional happy ending, I think the courage of the characters shines like the stars. (MH)

Cinderella

This story is told by the Native Peoples of North America. Many parts of this story are similar to the well-known European version—the cruel sisters, the downtrodden youngest daughter, and how she wins her prince in the end. This one has the interesting addition of the explanation of a natural feature—the aspen trees quivering. The source for this story is *Canadian Wonder Tales* by Cyrus Macmillan. (CS-C)

The Lake Lovers

I first met Maori stories in the beautiful collection by Kiri Te Kanawa: *Land of the Long White Cloud*, which includes this story in a longer and slightly different version. There is a fuller collection of Maori stories and songs in *The Maoris of New Zealand* by James Cowan. (MH)

Ned Kelly—Iron Man

The stories of Ned Kelly put him alongside Robin Hood and Dick Turpin as a glamorous rebel and an outlaw, breaking the law often for admired reasons such as helping the poor . . . Some say Ned was persecuted by the police from the start and never had a chance; others say that he was a plain criminal with no feelings for the law or for other people. There is probably some truth to both sides—but his was certainly a life of adventure. (CS-C)

The Missing Gold Coin

Stories of Nasrudin are told in many countries—India, Greece, Syria, and Turkey are just some of those where he is well known—and have been written down since at least the thirteenth century in what is now Iraq. The ending of this story—Nasrudin gaining the last gold coin—is my own invention. I have found several different tellings of this story. Sometimes they end two paragraphs before my ending, and sometimes they end with Nasrudin giving everything back to his neighbour. My story could have had another paragraph in which he does give everything back. It is, of course, still possible for him to give everything back as soon as they get home, and I think really that that is what he would have done, but I like my neat ending. The best collection of Nasrudin stories is sadly out of print: *Tales of the Hodja* retold by Charles Downing, published by Oxford University Press in 1964. (MH)

The Seven Baldies and One Shorty

Stories from Mongolia cover many familiar and unfamiliar themes, involving animals, gods, and humans. 'The reason why man became naked and the dog got his hair'; 'The blind frog in the well'; 'The nine sons of old Esguldei'; '10,000-year-old Tunjinkuu' are typical titles in a collection entitled *How Did the Great Bear Originate?* This story of the Baldies and Shorty is one of the more light-hearted ones. I am grateful to Munkhjargal Bilgoon for his help with source material from his native Mongolia. (CS-C)

The Barber's Wife

This story was told to Flora Annie Steel in north-west India. She went out to India in 1867, straight after her marriage at the age of 20. Her husband was an official but he couldn't cope with the heat and was constantly ill. Flora did his work for him, learnt the language, and talked to the people. She collected their stories and published them in a book in 1894. I have retold this story in my own words and left out the second half of the story in which the robbers try various tricks to get the gold coins. (MH)

Windy Stories

These tall stories are traditional in North America and can be found in many versions. I have retold them from *A Treasury of American Folklore* by B.A. Botkin (Crown Publishers, New York, 1944). These, and more, have also been used by Sid Fleischman in his *McBroom's Wonderful One-Acre Farm* and its sequels. (MH)

The Treasure Thief

This story of Ancient Egypt is only found in the great *History* by the Greek writer Herodotus. He was born in about 490 BC and went to Egypt doing the research for his book. He talked to many people and visited many places, and this is one of the stories he was told there. (MH)

The Blind Man, the Lame Man, and the Hunchback

This story shows that, even in a remote country such as the kingdom of Nepal, tales of giants, forests, and palaces are still told. Other well-loved stories from Nepal include 'The Story of the Much-Loved Diamond', 'Wasps versus Warriors'; and 'The Keeper of the Treasure'. I am grateful to Prince Nirajan of Nepal for his help over source material. (CS-C)

Momotaro the Peach Boy

As Japan is an island and is surrounded by other islands, many of the stories from there involve the sea. Rice is a staple food so the rice dumplings would have been an obvious food to give Momotaro as he set out. The peach to the Japanese represents long life and happiness—so this is why a hero such as Momotaro would be associated with the peach. Many Japanese stories involve everyday food, common animals, and the sea—stories such as 'My Lord Bag of Rice'; 'The Jelly-Fish and the Monkey'; 'The Happy Hunter and the Skilful Fisher'; and 'The White Hare and the Crocodiles'. (CS-C)

The Monkey and the Buddha

The 'Monkey King' is one of the best known figures in Chinese literature. He is the central character in a full length story called 'Journey to the West' in which he and his companion, Pig, have many adventures and come up against many challenges from both gods and men. Monkey is seen as the great optimist, with admirable determination to succeed and to overcome all odds—but on occasion, as in this story, the gods have other ideas. The full story, entitled *Monkey* by Wu Ch'Eng-En, is published by Penguin. (CS-C)

The Story of Da Trang and the Pearl

Many of the legends from Vietnam explain various features of nature. Other well known legends include 'How the Tiger Got Its Stripes'; 'Why Ducks Sleep Standing on one Leg'; 'The Gentleman of the Flies'; and 'The Toad is Heaven's Uncle'. The original version of this story explained that the little balls of sand you find on the beach in the early morning are made by crabs—and the soul of Da Trang has passed into these crabs, still trying to hold up the sea with sand. But it is really a story of the power of the sea over humans—even ones with magic powers.

I am grateful to Kate Silk for her help in finding source material for this story. (CS-C)

The Two Kings

Sundiata was a real king who defeated King Sumanguru at the great battle of Kirina in about 1240. The capital of his kingdom was on the headwaters of the great river Niger, at Sosso. He died in about 1260 and was remembered ever after as such a powerful king he must have been a man of magic. Stories grew up around him, as stories will, in many different versions. I have left out the great battle because I don't like battles, and I have made Sundiata himself discover the secret of the rooster's spur rather than one of his servants. I have also telescoped events, leaving out entirely the stories of Sundiata's years in exile. The complete story would be much too long for this book. I hope this version is true to the spirit of those who told his story around evening fires for hundreds of years. (MH)

Maria the Tall

Colombia, like much of South America, is full of jungle. Jungles have always been frightening and mysterious places for man to enter and explore. The idea of a presence that cannot be explained is a familiar one. Other stories from South America include animals and birds that are found in the jungle. I am grateful to Irene Vasco for assistance with source material and to Jethro Bennett for help with translation. (CS-C)

The illustrations are by:

Paul Dainton: pp71–74, 87–90, 111–118
Serena Feneziani: pp11–14, 35–40, 81–86, 105–110, 123–128
Liz Pyle: Cover illustrations, pp23–26, 41–46, 53–58, 137–140
Linda Schwab: pp15–22, 47–52, 59–64, 129–136
Sue Williams: pp27–34, 65–70, 95–104
Rosemary Woods: pp7–10, 75–80, 91–94, 119–122